# Advance praise for *Walker of Time*:

"This is a good story for young readers. . . . The author has done an excellent job of describing the environs of Walnut Canyon and of communicating Hopi life as an analogue of the ancient Sinagua. . . . Probably the greatest strength of the story is the portrayal of Hopi values."

**Peter J. Pilles, Jr.**
*Forest Archaeologist*
*Coconino National Forest*
*Flagstaff, Arizona*

"Children should really enjoy this book. It is a treat for the imagination. . . . I appreciate the attention and sensitivity to cultural and environmental values, the depiction of contrasts as well as similarities between ancient and modern life, and the friendship between the Hopi boy and the archaeologist's son. The message that friendship can span time and cultures is an important one."

**Dr. Connie Stone**
*Archaeologist*
*Phoenix, Arizona*

# Walker of Time

# WALKER
## OF
# TIME

## HELEN HUGHES VICK

*Harbinger House*
TUCSON

*To Howard and Mary Hughes
for their life-long love and support.*

*With special thanks to D. Ryan Carstens,
whose computer wizardry and
friendship made this book possible.*

HARBINGER HOUSE, INC.
Tucson, Arizona

Manufactured in the United States of America
∞ This book was printed on acid-free, archival-quality paper
*Editor:* Stacey Lynn
*Designer:* Harrison Shaffer

4 6 8 10 9 7 5 3

Library of Congress Cataloging-in-Publication Data
Vick, H. H. (Helen Hughes), 1950–
Walker of time / by H.H. Vick.
p. cm.
Summary: A fifteen-year-old Hopi boy and his freckled companion
travel back 800 years to the world of the Sinagua culture, a group
of people beset by drought and illness and in need of a leader.
ISBN 0-943173-84-1 (hc) —ISBN 0-943173-80-9 (paper)
1. Sinagua culture—Juvenile fiction. [1. Sinagua culture—
Fiction. 2. Hopi Indians—Fiction. 3. Indians of North America—
Fiction. 4. Time travel—Fiction. 5. Walnut Canyon National Monument
(Ariz.)—Fiction.] I. Title.
PZ7.V63Wal 1993
[Fic]—dc20 92-46740

# Preface

Walnut Canyon National Monument, just a few miles east of Flagstaff, Arizona, is a canyon shrouded in mystery. Tucked under its Kaibab limestone ledges are more than a hundred cliff ruins. These rooms made of mud and rock were the homes of an ancient culture that lived in the canyon more than nine hundred years ago. These prehistoric people thrived within the canyon walls until A.D. 1250, then very suddenly and mysteriously abandoned their comfortable rock homes to wind and time.

Since these ancient cliff dwellers were dry farmers, growing corn, beans, and squash, modern-day archaeologists have named them the "Sinagua." Sinagua is a Spanish word meaning "without water."

In 1915, Walnut Canyon was declared a national monument. By this time, unfortunately, many of the Sinagua ruins, artifacts, and burials sites had been looted by pot hunters or destroyed by curiosity seekers. Since 1915, many archaeological studies have been made at Walnut Canyon to learn more about the ancient ones called the Sinagua. Yet these studies haven't answered the two most important questions concerning the Sinagua: Why did they leave? Where did they go? Walnut Canyon's mysteries are yet to be solved.

# 1

Walker's lungs were burning. The muscles in his legs were cramping up in pain with each pounding stride up the steep, narrow trail. His nose and throat felt as if they had been sandpapered raw from the dust that he kicked up in little puffs with each step. The water jug's thick leather strap, hanging over his bare right shoulder, bit deep into his skin with each movement. Water sloshed out of the heavy, old ceramic jug, sending small streams of water trickling down his reddish-brown back. Sweat ran off Walker's high, broad forehead into his dark brown eyes. The sweat mixed with his tears and blurred his vision. Without slowing his pace, Walker reached up and wiped the salty mixture out of his puffy eyes.

The well-used path came to an abrupt turn. Switching back in the other direction, it traversed the steep side of the northern Arizona mesa. Walker's worn jogging shoes slipped from underneath him. He fought to regain his balance. Water gushed out of the jug, down his back, and onto his faded blue gym shorts. He went down on one knee, hitting the rocky path. Walker felt the skin on his knee and palms scraping off as he skidded to a stop.

Walker's panting turned into a deep sob. His strong shoulders shook. Clenching his fist in anger, he struck the ground where he crouched on one knee. Water spilled over his shoulder and down his muscular chest.

"He can't die! He can't go and leave me totally alone!" Walker cried, hitting the ground again. Even as his ears heard these words, his heart tightened with a deep sorrow that confirmed what his mind knew to be true. Náat, his uncle, the only family Walker had known in his fifteen years of life, was dying.

Walker struggled to his feet. His entire body screamed with pain from running the three miles down the mesa to the spring and jogging back up the steep trail with the full water jug. But the pain his body felt was nothing compared to the agony that tore at his heart.

Wiping his bloody hands on his shorts, then using the back of his hand to clear the tears from his eyes, Walker started up the trail again. His short, muscular legs pumped as hard and fast as they could.

Cresting the mesa's flat, rocky rim, Walker slowed his pace. Wiping his eyes again and straightening his shoulders, he tried to calm his thoughts and feelings. With quick strides, he moved along the rim of the mesa toward his Hopi village. His heart beat against his ribs with such painful fury that he had to stop to fight for his breath.

The sunset painted the Arizona sky blood red as Walker stood on the edge of the mesa. He gazed toward the San Francisco Peaks. Well over ninety miles away, the sacred mountain could be seen clearly from the mesa's rim.

"Each morning with the first rays of your light, I have come here with Náat to pray to you, Taawa, our creator," whispered Walker in a broken voice. "Each day, I have looked at the sacred peaks where the holy spirits of the Hopi people live. Each day I have found peace and harmony in seeing the three sacred peaks on the horizon. But not now, not today. Náat is dying! Soon his spirit will become a cloud and travel to Maski, the house of the dead, where his spirit will live forever." Walker beat his clenched fist against his bare leg. "And I—I will be alone!"

Walker looked down over the rocky cliffs of the mesa onto the vast desert floor below. The white man's paved, black roads crisscrossed Hopi like long streaks of lightning. His eyes fell on the white man's school where he had been forced to learn the bahana's language and ways.

*What good are the bahana's ways?* Walker thought with anger. *Their ways only destroy the traditional way—the Hopi way. Even their great medical knowledge can't save Náat from the cold fingers of the god of death, Masau'u.*

Walker turned to face his seven hundred-year-old village. It looked like an ancient bahana's motel with its long sections of straight walls containing six or seven individual doors. Much like the bahana's motels, all the long rows of adobe homes were built around a large center area, the plaza. The bahana's heated swimming pool would sit in the middle of the plaza, Walker thought, scrutinizing his village. Yes, the village was like a motel except that it lacked such basic comforts as running water, central heating or air conditioning, and of course, flushing toilets. He had to chuckle at that thought.

The flat roofs of the old, one-story pueblo dwellings mirrored the great flat-top mountains on which they were

3

built. The homes' thick rock-and-mortar walls blended into the rocky cliffs of the mesa so well that from the desert below the village was all but invisible.

For hundreds of years the Hopi villages on top of three different mesas had remained relatively untouched in their ancient ways. Even when the bahanas did come, the Hopi people had stubbornly clung to their old ways. It had been only in the last ten years that electrical poles had been planted next to some of the ancient dwellings.

Walker remembered well how he had begged Náat for electricity that could bring bright light into their dark, one-room home, not to mention the wonders of the bahana's television!

"You must let the old ways light your life, filling your heart and mind," Náat had replied, looking deep into Walker's eyes.

"Then why must I go to the bahana's school each day?" Walker countered with a scowl.

"You must learn the bahana's ways so that you can help your people survive in the old ways." Náat closed his eyes. His lips pulled together in a tight line as if he knew that what he had just said was a contradiction, if not an impossibility. Opening his eyes, he stated firmly, "You will have great need for the old ways and the bahana's way. You will learn both."

Walker had gone to the bahana's school each day for the last nine years and had learned what the white man felt he needed to know. He worked hard and excelled in all subjects, especially sports. Each day after school, Walker returned home to live in the traditional ways.

Náat was a loving teacher but demanded much more

from Walker than any of the bahana teachers at school did. Sitting by Náat's feet, Walker learned hundreds of the old legends and how their moral principles shaped his life. He learned the traditional way of doing everything from cooking to singing the sacred prayer songs. In the summers, Walker worked side by side with Náat in their fields. He learned and relearned all the skillful ways of planting and growing the corn, squash, and beans that they lived on through the winter. Náat pushed him relentlessly to learn to hunt with great skill and accuracy, first with a rabbit stick, then with a bow and arrow. He taught Walker independence by giving him plenty of responsibilities, many of which were above Walker's capabilities. Walker learned to extend himself to meet these challenges.

Walker could not remember the time when he didn't feel as if he were walking on a tightrope. He had to continually struggle to maintain a balance between the bahana's ways and demands and the traditional ways that Náat lived and taught. None of his friends' parents seemed so intent on their children learning the bahana's ways while insisting that they live in the old ways. Only Náat seemed to demand the impossible, and it was Náat who taught Walker to walk in balance between the two seemingly opposite life-styles.

Now, watching the evening light wash his village in a pinkish color, Walker whispered, "Náat, after you are gone, who will guide and help me find harmony between the bahana's and the old ways?" Already, he felt abandoned.

Taking swift steps, Walker went past the first section of homes. His ears filled with the familiar sounds of children playing, babies crying, dogs barking, men talking, and women visiting. Not wanting to speak to anyone, Walker kept his eyes down. He passed many, but because he did not meet their eyes, none spoke.

Walker slipped in between the walls of two homes that formed a narrow passageway that led into the plaza. The rasping sound of corn being ground on an ancient grinding stone echoed off the close walls. A shiver raced up Walker's back. His sweaty body felt like ice. He had heard this sound every day of his life, but at this minute it suddenly took on a new meaning.

*Red cornmeal,* Walker thought, hurrying past the open door of the grinding room. *I must grind red corn into meal to leave at Náat's grave.*

Walker's heart was pounding with anxious fear as he opened the heavy, old, weathered door of Náat's one-room home. The smell of sickness and approaching death filled the cool room. The small, cracked window pane let in just enough fading light for Walker to see that Náat's eyes were closed, but his chest slowly lifted the thin wool blanket that covered him.

Walker let out his breath with relief. He hadn't wanted to leave Náat even for a few minutes, but they had needed water, which meant hiking down to the spring and hauling the water back before dark.

"Taawa, thank you for staying Masau'u's deathly fingers till I came back," Walker prayed in silence.

With soft steps, Walker went to the front corner of the room that served as the kitchen. He lit the old, tarnished kerosene lamp that hung from the open wood beam in the ceiling. Its dull light spread long, dark shadows across the room. He poured some water from the jug into the chipped, white enamel bowl sitting on the small wooden table. As he dipped his hands into the large bowl, his scraped palms stung. Biting his lower lip, Walker washed the dirt and blood off his hands. He splashed his face with water, rinsing away the streaks of tears and sweat.

He poured water into one of the two cracked plastic cups that were stacked neatly on the table next to two tin plates and two mismatched sets of eating utensils. Taking the full cup, Walker moved the ten feet to the back of the room where Náat's narrow bed stood. The only chair in the house stood next to the bed. The wooden chair squeaked and wobbled under Walker's weight as he sat down on it.

Náat's eyes opened. He looked toward Walker. "Wayma?" Náat said in his native tongue, calling Walker by his Hopi name. His voice was a mere whisper.

"I am here, Náat. I had to go for water. I knew you would be thirsty when you woke up." Putting his arm under Náat's thin shoulders, Walker helped him into a sitting position.

Náat's bony fingers held the cup to his pale lips. He drank in small, shallow sips. His wrinkled face was pinched with pain and weakness.

"Wayma, we must talk," Náat said, easing back down on the coverless pillow. His crooked fingers reached up to touch the eagle-shaped pendant that lay on his withered chest. Strung on a worn leather thong, it had been cut from a seashell and inlaid with tiny rectangular pieces of turquoise. It had hung around Náat's neck as long as Walker could remember.

"You must rest," Walker said, his throat tightening.

"It is time that you wear the pendant of our brother, the eagle," Náat said, straining to untie the thong's knot.

Walker shook his head. "I can't. It's yours." Walker felt

his chin tremble. Tears threatened his eyes. "It will always be yours."

The thong slipped off in Náat's dark hand. "No, it is not mine. It has always been yours, Wayma. I was told to wear it until you needed it, and that time is now." With his hand shaking, Náat held the eagle pendant out toward Walker. "You must wear it—always."

Walker swallowed hard and took the pendant into his own quivering hand. He looked down at it. A tear splashed on the small blue bits of turquoise.

"Now I must tell one more story," Náat's voice had an urgent tone to it.

Walker's heart tightened. Somehow he knew that this would be his uncle's last story. He fought back the tears stinging his eyes.

"Long ago, when I was young and strong like you," Náat paused, lost in the memory of long-ago youth, "my uncles and grandfather took me in a wagon to a canyon southeast of the holy peaks. Eagles nested in the high cliffs. We needed eaglets. These sacred young would be taken back to the village and raised as our own in the Hopi way. Their feathers would be used for pahos, our holy prayer sticks. The canyon was full of the rock houses built in the cliffs by the ancient ones." Náat closed his dark, sunken eyes.

Walker studied Náat's face. The once proud and smiling face was a deathly gray in the lantern's stark light. The many wrinkles of time seemed to form deep ravines in the dark, weathered skin.

The old eyes opened. From the sound of Náat's voice, Walker knew that he was struggling. "We went down into the canyon, past many cliff houses of the ancient ones. All the houses were empty except for wind, memories—magic. We hunted and hunted, but we found only one eaglet. My grandfather said that we must go in different directions to find more. I hiked west into a finger of the canyon. There I found a narrow path that many had traveled long ago." Again Náat stopped. His cough was becoming deeper. Beads of sweat danced on his wrinkled forehead.

"Clouds came from the holy mountain and covered the sky, making it very dark. Then the lightning came with great thunder. Rain started to fall in big drops. Lightning was all around me. I saw a cave, so I went in. In the cave was a shrine, a Hopi shrine—yet not Hopi. There was a paho on the shrine. I picked up the prayer stick. Great thunder filled the cave." Náat's thin body shook with another deep cough. He fought for breath.

"Rest," Walker said, holding Náat's bony hand. He felt Náat's brittle fingers try to squeeze his hand.

"Get the backpack," Náat whispered, looking toward Walker's old, canvas backpack sitting on the floor at the end of the bed.

Walker rose and took the few steps to the pack. Reaching down to pick it up, he realized that he had not seen the old pack in more than a year. Lifting it up, he could tell that something was inside. The pack wasn't heavy, just awkward.

"I will open it for you," Walker said, laying the backpack beside Náat.

Náat raised his hand a few inches off the bed. "No! Open it at the cave. The bahanas call the canyon Walnut Canyon. They made it a national monument to keep the homes of the old ones safe." Náat's glassy eyes stared at Walker. "Go to this canyon. Find the cave. Must be in the

9

cave when sun is highest, on last day of the hunter's moon."
A series of deep coughs shook Náat's weathered body. His
breath came in short, raspy wheezes. His eyes filled with an
intenseness that Walker had never seen before. "In cave . . .
open pack . . . Walk time . . . Time very short . . . Walk
time, Wayma . . . Do what must be done . . . Come home . . .
to Hopi."

# 2

Walker brushed the long strand of blue-black hair out of his eyes. The breeze that blew up out of the canyon had unseasonably cold fingers that seemed to be pulling at his life's breath. A chill crawled up his spine and pulled at the hairs on his neck.

He leaned on the iron railing that encircled the lookout point. The metal felt cold, clammy. Walker's eyes searched the canyon below. A sea of slate gray clouds filled the six-hundred-foot-deep canyon. Only the first hundred feet of the rocky limestone cliffs were visible above the cloud level. The sky overhead matched the clouds below. The late August air smelled of rain.

Walker's hand reached up and touched the eagle-shaped pendant that now hung around his neck on the worn leather thong. An ache deep within his chest worked its way up to his throat. Walker tried to swallow the ache. His hand tightened on the timeworn turquoise pendant.

*Náat, I have come as you wanted. Is your spirit one of the clouds covering the canyon, waiting for me to come down among the ruins? Or is your spirit already at Maski, the house of the dead?*

Another cold breeze from within the canyon seemed to pull at him. He let go of the cold iron railing. The distant sound of thunder rolled off the San Francisco Peaks to the northwest.

"What must I do here among the ruins of the ancient ones that the bahanas call the Sinagua?" Walker asked the clouds. The only answer he heard was the wind's song as it rushed through the surrounding pines.

Walker moved to the paved trail head a few feet away and looked down. The path of cement stairs that led down to the ancient ones' ruins disappeared into a blanket of dark clouds. A bahana with an expensive camera around his neck and wearing gray running shoes appeared, trotting up the stairs. He was followed by a chunky, blond-haired boy, who was carrying a can of pop and a half-eaten bag of potato chips.

"I didn't think I'd ever make it out of there," huffed the boy, climbing up the last step. He stopped next to Walker to catch his breath. After a few big gulps of air, he said to Walker, "Two hundred and fifty stairs up and down!" Putting a handful of chips into his mouth and munching, he looked back down the path. "It is weird down there," he said, still chewing. "Going through all those cliff ruins is just like walking back in time hundreds of years."

"Come on, son. We've got to hurry. Got to make it to the Grand Canyon by five," the boy's father said, still hurrying up the path toward the Visitor Center.

The boy shrugged his shoulders, took a big gulp of his drink and lumbered after his father. "Good luck down there," he called, looking back at Walker. "Hope you make it out."

Walker smiled, adjusted the backpack on his shoulders, and stepped down the first of the two hundred and fifty steps. A bolt of lightning flashed down to the rocky rim across the canyon. The thunder that followed was deafening.

Walker climbed down the first set of ten stairs onto a narrow paved trail. His eyes scanned the metal Park Service sign standing at the edge of the path. "In Case of Thunderstorms Take Shelter in the Ruins," it stated.

Lightning illuminated the darkened sky. Thunder roared in response.

A few feet further down Walker stopped to read a second sign. "The Sinagua Indians left Walnut Canyon about A.D. 1250. No one knows why they left the area. No one knows where they went."

An uneasy feeling started in the pit of Walker's stomach and traveled up into his chest. His heart pumped the feeling to the rest of his body.

Walker continued down the winding path through giant limestone boulders and ponderosa pine trees. As he climbed down the third set of stairs, the clouds seemed to swallow him. The air felt thick and clammy. A shudder traversed up his back.

Holding on to the metal railing, Walker hurried down the next set of stairs. At the base of the stairs the path wound around a huge boulder with a tree growing in the middle of it. The scrawny pinyon pine clung stubbornly to the rock, its branches reaching for the sky.

"Hohu," Walker whispered, looking at the tree. "You and I are alike. I, too, exist in a hard place, stuck between the bahana's world and the old traditional ways of my people."

A jet's engine roared as it raced across the sky above. Walker looked up but couldn't see the jet, the sky, or the rim of the canyon. The thick, dark clouds wrapped above him like a low ceiling. The wind's pull was stronger. An ear-shattering roll of thunder drowned the jet's roar.

Rubbing the eagle pendant with his fingers, Walker continued his journey down the path of many steps. With each step down, he felt more and more cut off from the world of cars, jets, and computers above him.

Without warning, Walker came upon the first set of cliff ruins, nestled under a deep, cavelike, limestone overhang. A long rock-and-mud wall stretched the length of the overhang. He could see four separate doorways in the ancient wall.

The cold August wind whipped at Walker's face. Its chilled fingers once again seemed to pull at his very being. Tears from the wind's cold bite filmed over Walker's eyes. A strange, unnameable feeling swept over him like a wave.

"You have stood here before," the feeling stated.

Walker shook himself, like a dog shaking off water. "No. In all of my fifteen years, I have never been here before," he whispered to the wind. Thunder filled the air with vibrations as it echoed off the canyon walls.

Walker stood looking at the four-foot-thick wall. He could tell that much time and great effort had been spent making this wall that had stood for at least eight hundred years. Each flat, limestone rock had been cut, laid, and mortared with great skill. The T-shaped doorway into each dwelling was a mere two feet wide.

The ancient ones must have been short like the Hopi, Walker realized as he stood in front of the middle door. Judging by the height of the doorway, the ancient ones couldn't have been any taller than five feet three or four inches.Walker tucked his shoulders down, bent at the waist, and put his hands on the short rock ledges at each side of the door. His palms felt the smooth, well-worn rocks. How many people have placed their hands here to get into this room? Walker wondered, crawling into the dark ruin.

An acrid smell of age and death filled Walker's nose as his eyes adjusted to the semidarkness. The strange feeling again swept over him, whispering, "You know this place."

Automatically Walker's hand reached up and clasped the eagle pendant. The whispery feeling slipped away.

The side walls that separated this room from the others were made of the same stone-and-mud mortar as the front wall. Walker could see that the very low ceiling and the back wall were formed by the limestone overhang. Black soot from ancient fires stained the ceiling in one corner of the ruin. The floor was hard-packed dirt.

Looking closer at a side wall, Walker realized that it had been plastered with a layer of mud. He moved to the front wall next to the doorway where the light was better. A shiver shook his body. He could see handprints in the primitive mud plaster. They seemed to be small, like women's hands.

"All except this one," Walker exclaimed, reaching up to a print just above his eye level. "This one's palm is wide, the fingers long and slim." Walker slipped his man-sized hand into the misfit print. The fingers of the dateless print were a good inch and a half longer than his.

The mysterious feeling grasped Walker. This time he let it wash over him. He closed his eyes. The haunting feeling swirled around and through him.

His nose filled with the smell of ancient smoke. It seemed that smoke curled around his face, drifting toward the air vents at the top of the doorway.

Memories hidden deep within his being seemed to take over Walker's mind. He saw the glow of a small fire in the corner. Two people huddled close to the flaming warmth. One rocked back and forth, cradling an infant in her arms. Distantly familiar yet strange-sounding words and rhythm flowed through the air with the ancient smoke. Walker focused on the words, trying to make sense of them.

> *"May you live many years.*
> *May you have good crops of corn.*
> *May you have good health. . . . "*

A clap of thunder shook the darkened walls. Walker drew his hand out of the strange mud print and opened his eyes to the empty ruin.

# 3

Using the stone door ledges, Walker crawled out of the ancient ruin. The cold, humid air cleared his head. Goose bumps rose on his sweaty skin. Clutching the eagle pendant, he drew in a deep breath of cold air, then another and another. His knees felt like jelly.

"What magic is this?" Walker whispered to the wind. "Why am I here? What must I do?"

Walker looked at his digital watch. Eleven fifteen. He had forty-five minutes to find the cave. Why in the last minutes of Náat's life had time become so important to him? wondered Walker. Náat had never been concerned about the white man's concept of time before. How many times had he said, "The Hopi's way is not concerned with hours, days, or years. The Hopi way is concerned only with living with peace within ourselves and with those around us. Think happy thoughts, good thoughts; time will take care of itself."

Lightning flashed in the cloud-darkened sky. Thunder shook the air around Walker, bringing his mind back to the present. He wiped away the tears that clouded his eyes.

Think happy thoughts, good thoughts, as Náat taught, Walker told himself. He started up the paved path past the ancient one's home. He chuckled. *Maybe I won't get back to Hopi in time to start school next week!*

Walker stopped in front of a large ruin containing eight good-sized rooms. He let his eyes search the trees and bushes below the paved trail. Within seconds, he saw a narrow, unused path that led down the side of the canyon and disappeared into a large stand of juniper pines. Walker smiled, remembering how helpful the Park Ranger at the Visitor Center had been earlier that day.

"Yes, there is a cave in the canyon," the red-haired ranger had said, looking at him with sudden interest. "Not many people know about it since it's not on the paved trail that goes around the ruins. It's about here," he said, pointing to a park map hanging on the wall behind him. "The trail to it starts just below the largest group of ruins." He leaned a few inches toward Walker. "No one is allowed in that area. It is restricted. You must stay on the paved trail," the ranger stated, looking Walker straight in the eye.

Now Walker quickly checked the paved trail for tourists. Only the wind traveled the blacktop path, rushing in and out of the rock ruins.

"Well I am *no one*," Walker told the wind. He left the bahana's paved trail and climbed down to the unused path below.

The steep, narrow path was worn deep into the hard earth. "Many traveled the path long ago . . ." Náat's words echoed in Walker's memory. Thunder rolled off the rim into the canyon.

Walker followed the path eastward through pine trees, sagebrush, cactus, skunk bush, and limestone boulders down the side of the rocky canyon. After about ten minutes of climbing downward, Walker felt that he should be getting close to the floor of the canyon. Within a minute he came to a fork in the path. Wiping his brow, he stopped and studied the two paths. The main path probably continued down to the stream of water in the bottom of the canyon. The smaller path that branched off to the west must go to the cave, Walker figured, shifting his backpack on his shoulders. A long roll of thunder seemed to confirm his thoughts.

Walker checked his digital watch. Thirty-three minutes left. He started up the rocky path. He hummed an age-old song that Náat had always sung while working in his corn fields. "Music lightens the heart and body," Náat had told him many times. "Songs are prayers, too."

The rocky path led up the side of the canyon for a hundred feet. Continuing, it traversed the side of the rugged canyon along a limestone ledge for another mile, then climbed sharply upward.

The wind beat against Walker's face. Thunder rolled off one canyon wall and echoed off the opposite wall. Walker checked his watch. Ten minutes to twelve. How much farther? His legs ached from the hard climbing; his stomach growled from hunger. He kept his strong, short legs moving.

Without warning, the path came to an abrupt end. Walker stood at the edge of the sheer drop-off and looked down. He could see no way down the cliff's steep face. He looked above him. The limestone rose straight up a good hundred feet. Climbing up seemed impossible.

Doubts clouded Walker's mind. He must have taken the wrong path. Maybe there's more than one cave. What was he doing here, anyway? What could he possibly do in an old cave? *Why, Náat? Why here, of all places?* Walker stood looking at the cliff as the minutes flew by. He closed his eyes and took a deep breath, trying to calm his thoughts. A desperate feeling began to seep into his heart.

"Taawa, my creator, help me find my way," pleaded Walker, looking into the dark clouds overhead.

Lightning raced out of the clouds, almost striking the top of a single pine tree growing on a rocky ledge a good ten feet above and to the right of Walker's head. In the bright flash, he saw a dark opening in the limestone wall almost directly behind the tree.

Walker's heart raced. He searched the limestone for a crack or crevice that he could use as a handhold. His fingertips found a grooved hole in the cliff's face. As he pulled himself up, he spotted another worn groove just above his eye level. His foot slipped into a small toe-notch. The ancient ones had carved a path up to the cave! With care, he started to scale the sheer limestone wall to the narrow ledge above.

With a final heave, Walker pulled himself up and onto the six-foot-deep ledge. Huge drops of rain washed his face. Lightning licked the sky like a snake's long, forked tongue. Thunder rolled like great, endless waves in the air.

"Taawa, thank you," Walker shouted over the thunder.

The large pine tree stood about a foot and a half in front of the cave. The mouth of the cave was only three or four inches taller than Walker and only a few feet wide. Cold, moist air met Walker's nose as he entered the darkened cave. It took only a few seconds for his eyes to adjust. The cave's back wall was just a few feet from the entrance. Standing in the middle of the cave, he could almost touch the side walls. From the amount of light in the cave now, Walker realized that on a good day sunlight would flood the cave.

Hearing a hollow, dripping sound, Walker pulled his pencil-sized flashlight from the back pocket of his blue jeans. He shined the flashlight's strong beam toward the back of the cave and quickly spotted the source of the sound. From a crack in the limestone ceiling, drops of water fell into a small pool below. Walker moved to the pool and knelt down. He could see that from years of the water dripping, a natural basin had been formed in the limestone. Green moss edged the rim of the basin.

Walker dipped his cupped hands into the pool. The water was ice cold. Lifting his hands to his mouth, he took a big sip. The haunting feeling washed over him.

"You have drunk here before," it whispered.

A flash of lightning lit the cave. Looking up, Walker saw the shrine. It was on a natural rock ledge two feet above and to the right of the small pool of water. A cold chill shook his body.

Walker aimed his light up onto the rock shrine. He had seen many similar shrines around his village, and each year he had helped his uncle neatly stack rocks to form such a shrine in their cornfield. On these shrines he had placed pahos, the holy prayer feathers, and fine cornmeal as offerings to the supernatural powers. Each year rains were sent to the field.

Walker stood up for a closer look at the shrine. It was almost identical to a Hopi shrine, yet different. The exact placement and slant of each rock were not the same as in the Hopi way. Studying the shrine, he realized that after hundreds of years it was barren; there were no offerings.

"Open the backpack in the cave," Náat's words exploded in Walker's memory.

Kneeling down, Walker took off his backpack and placed it in front of him. Thunder shook the walls of the cave. He unbuckled the top of the pack and pulled back the top flap. Inside was an object about eight inches long, wrapped in a piece of white buckskin. Walker lifted it out and unwrapped the soft skin.

His racing heart tightened as he looked at the paho lying in his trembling hands. The two distinctively carved pieces of wood were tied together with a thread-thin strand of leather. Each piece of wood had a carved face: the left a male, the right a female. White eagle feathers surrounded the images. The paho looked Hopi; yet like the shrine it was not Hopi.

It was centuries old, Walker realized, gently turning the paho over in his hands to inspect it. The wood felt as fragile as fine glass that would crumble under even the slightest pressure. The feathers, though intact, looked as if one breath of air would disintegrate them.

"So, Náat, this is why you sent me here," Walker said in a low voice. "Years ago you took this paho from the shrine." Walker shook his head. He couldn't imagine why his uncle had removed the sacred prayer stick from its rightful place.

Standing up, Walker stated, "It doesn't matter why you did, Náat. I will do what must be done—I will replace the paho." He reached over to lay the prayer stick on the shrine.

The sound of rolling rocks startled him. Holding the paho inches above the shrine, Walker jerked his head backward. His eyes searched the mouth of the cave. A brilliant flash of lightning lit the cave's entrance. In that split second, a head of curly, dark brown hair appeared. It was followed by a long, thin body rolling into the cave. A lean, freckled face looked up at Walker in surprise, and a toothy grin streaked across the face.

The entire cave exploded with thunder. The deafening sound echoed through Walker's head, piercing his brain with pain.

Total darkness consumed the cave. The air felt heavy with age, decay, and death. The cave seemed to shake, twist, turn, swirl. Walker fell to his knees. The sharp, rocky floor bit into his skin.

Thunder shook his body in great waves. The air seemed to get heavier, thicker, harder to breathe. Walker gasped for a breath. None would come. The cave twisted, twirled, and swirled faster and faster.

He felt his leaden body slumping forward, his cheek striking the wall of the cave as he hit the hard ground. Yet the sensation of endless floating seem to lift him up into the thick darkness.

"Air . . . Can't breathe . . . Need air . . . Great Taawa help me!" Walker's mind cried. Endless darkness swirled around and around.

# 4

Warmth licked at his stinging cheek. Warmth filled his cold body, but Walker couldn't get his eyelids to open.

"Hey, wake up. Are you okay?" Walker could hear. The strange voice sounded a thousand miles away. Its words traveled on thunder.

"Come on. You have to wake up." Whoever was talking started to shake Walker's shoulder. "Wake up!"

Walker tried to focus his thoughts. His mind seemed to be floating in and out of time.

"Here, have some water," said the voice. Walker felt ice water flooding over his cheeks and into his nose. His eyes flew open, his mouth gasping for air. Coughing racked his body.

"There. You're okay—you're okay. The old water trick works every time," said the strange voice with a nervous laugh. "Some storm eh? I've never seen thunder and lightning like that before. Thought I was going to get fried any minute. That last big thunder blast all but knocked me out, too. It shook the cave like an earthquake. Really strange. Do you want to sit up?" the voice asked.

Walker let the arms attached to the voice help him to a sitting position. The coughing stopped. He could breathe again.

He looked at the voice's body. A vague memory of the face formed in his mind. It was the same lean, very freckled face that had smiled at him just before the cave had exploded with thunder. The face was framed with wild, dark, curly brown hair. Light brown eyes shone with relief as they looked down at him. The full lips spread into the same giant, toothy grin.

"Am I glad that you're all right!" said the boy, who seemed to be about eleven or twelve years old. He was a good four inches taller than Walker. "You are all right, aren't you? Do you want to stand up?"

Walker shook his head. Pain thundered inside of it. He reached up to touch it but found the paho was still in his right hand.

"Here, let me get you some more water," said the boy, moving toward the pool and dipping his large freckled hands into it. Looking at the water dribbling out between his long fingers, he asked, "How about if I just help you get over to the pool?" Gently but firmly, he helped Walker half scoot, half crawl the foot or so to the edge of the pool.

Walker cupped his hand and dipped it into the pool. The water's coldness shot through his body like lightning. His head cleared and focused sharply. He looked around the cave. It was bathed in sunlight. The air smelled different somehow.

"You're looking better already. What's your name? You're Indian, aren't you?" the boy said.

Walker looked at the fast-talking boy. His freckled face was one big grin. He knew that the bahana meant no insult by the question.

"Hopi," said Walker.

"What village are you from?"

Walker took a second look at this friendly bahana. Not many whites knew that there were different villages at Hopi.

Walker answered, "Mishongnovi."

"Second Mesa, eh? The one by Corn Rock, right? I went to one of your religious Kachina dances in July. It sure was hot. I couldn't believe there's only one pop machine in all of Hopi and absolutely no place to get pizza. I thought I was going to die!" the boy said, shaking his curly head.

Walker took another drink from the pool. His mind was full of questions. But he knew if he just waited, all would be answered.

"My name is Trumount Abraham Grotewald, but everyone calls me Tag," stated the boy, plopping down next to Walker. "You're about fifteen years old, right?"

Walker nodded. Pain raced through his brain.

"I'm twelve, tall for my age, and my Mom says I'm twelve going on twenty. That's because I'm an only child, I guess. Anyway, my Dad is the archaeologist here at Walnut Canyon. We live in a trailer on the rim of the canyon. I'd like to live in town, but Dad says he needs to be close to his work. That's all he ever talks about—'dead Indians.'" Tag looked apologetically at Walker. "No offense meant. It's just that my Dad eats, drinks, and sleeps archaeology. He doesn't like sports or even television. Crazy, eh? I mean that's *all* he does is archaeology. Sometimes I get pretty sick of it all." Tag shrugged his broad, bony shoulders.

"Anyway, that's why I'm here. He said he was going to

start a dig in the cave for some new study." Tag's face broke into his giant grin. He reached into his T-shirt pocket and held out a silver compass. "I decided I'd come up here first and bury my compass here in the cave." He chuckled. "Won't that just kill my Dad when he digs up an official Boy Scout compass in this ancient Sinagua cave? Great, eh?" Tag looked at Walker. His grin faded.

"Well anyway, just call me Tag." He stuck out his hand to shake.

Walker looked at the huge, outstretched, freckled hand. Why did all bahanas want to shake hands? he wondered. Ignoring the bahana's hand, he stared into the pool.

After a few seconds, Tag dropped his hand into his lap. "You haven't told me your name."

"Qeni Wayma Talayesva," Walker said, looking up at Tag. In spite of himself, he felt his mouth turn up in a smile. "You bahanas call me Walker."

Tag chuckled. "I can see why. Your name is as bad as mine!"

Laughing too, Walker started to stand up. His legs were still weak. He sat back down.

"Still wobbly, eh? Better rest a minute more before we climb out of here. Boy, am I glad I found the cave when I did. I've never seen lightning up that close before. A big bolt of it hit the tree out in front just as I rolled inside," said Tag, pointing to the mouth of the cave. His eyes grew large. Scrambling to his feet, he hurried to the cave's entrance.

"The tree is totally gone," he exclaimed, turning back to look at Walker. "There's not even a trace of it left!"

His head pounding with each step, Walker made his way to the entrance. The ledge was barren; not even a single blade of beeweed grew in the many cracks of the limestone. The high noon sun shone brightly. A raven floated in the air above, screeching.

"This is weird." Tag ran his hands through his curly hair.

Walker scanned the narrow ledge. "There are no rain puddles."

"You're right." Tag knelt down and touched the pitted and cracked limestone. "It's not even damp. In fact, it's hot. The rain was coming down in buckets when I finally made it into the cave. Now there's not a trace." Looking at his wrist watch, he said, "My watch stopped at 12:00, so I'm not sure what time it is now. I must have been knocked unconscious, too. We must have been out a couple of hours at least."

Walker didn't answer. He stood looking down at the canyon. "Longer than that, I think. Look," Walker said, pointing downward with his chin.

Tag's mouth fell open, and his big eyes grew even larger. The familiar canyon looked alien. No longer were there thick growths of juniper, ponderosa, pinyon pine, and Douglas fir trees covering the sides. Instead, rugged layers of multicolored limestone lay bare in the bright sun. Only small, squatty bunches of sage and cactus grew here and there. Even the cactus looked dry and parched. The air seemed different, too. It was cleaner, fresher, yet hotter and drier—harsher.

"Something is definitely wrong," Tag stated. He sat down on the ledge, letting his long legs dangle down into midair.

Walker sat down next to Tag. "Not wrong, just different."

The silence that followed was broken by the sound of a black raven's screeching laugh. The mysterious feeling once again filled Walker. Goose bumps rose up all over his body.

"Walk time . . . Walk time," it whispered.

Walker reached up and grasped the eagle pendant around his neck. *Walk time*. Náat had used those same words.

"Walk time," whispered Walker, his eyes searching the canyon below.

"What?" asked Tag, turning to look at him. "Walk time?"

"Yes. We have walked time." Seeing the look of bewilderment on Tag's freckled face, Walker stood up. "Come on." He turned and went back inside the cave.

"The shrine," said Walker, pointing to the ledge above the pool. "When I came in, before the lightning hit, it was empty—abandoned. But look at it now."

On the ledge next to the rock shrine stood a medium-sized, white ceramic bowl with black lightning-like designs on it. The bowl was about a third full of fine, white cornmeal. Next to the bowl lay two carved sticks tied together with a thin leather thong. Eagle feathers adorned the sticks.

"Wow! I was so busy trying to wake you up that I didn't even notice the shrine. Hey! I've seen that bowl before. It's one of the Sinagua pots in the display case at the Visitor Center. My Dad said it was a religious offering bowl of some kind. What is it doing here?"

"Making an offering," answered Walker in a low tone.

Tag's voice sounded nervous, "Who would do such a dumb thing?"

"The ones who built the shrine."

"Look, that's a prayer stick, isn't it?" asked Tag, pointing to the wood-and-feather effigy beside the bowl.

Walker nodded, his eyes fastened on the paho in his own hand.

"Hey, you've got one almost like it!" exclaimed Tag. "Where did you . . ." Confusion spread across his freckled face. He put his hands on his waist. "What is going on here?"

"We have walked time back to the ancient ones," Walker answered.

"You're telling me that somehow we have been zapped back in time more than seven hundred years to the Sinagua's time? Oh come on, get serious," Tag said with a laugh. The strained sound echoed off the narrow walls of the cave and died. He shifted from one big foot to the other. "But how? Why?" he asked in almost a whisper.

"I'm not sure. The paho. The thunder and lightning. Magic." Walker looked at Tag. "All I know is that I was sent here for a reason. 'Do what must be done,' my uncle said. At first I thought it was just to put the paho back." Walker took a deep breath and held it a few seconds. "But now, I know there is more that must be done. And for some reason time is running out."

"Just a minute. All of this is just too much. I don't understand any of it!" Tag shouted. Shaking his head in disbelief, he stalked out of the cave.

Walker picked up the white piece of buckskin from where it had fallen on the cave floor. He carefully rewrapped the paho. Something deep inside told him that it was not the time to put it back on the shrine. Retrieving his backpack, he threw the flap open and looked inside. A piece of light brown buckskin met his eyes.

Unfolding the smooth, soft skin he realized it was a pair of leggings. Sewn down the outside seam of each leg was a line of small, white seashells. The narrow waist was tied with a thong of heavy leather. A new pair of soft, dark moccasins was wrapped inside.

Setting the clothes down, Walker reached in the pack and lifted out the last item. It was an old, cloth bag that flour had come in many years ago. A heavy piece of cotton string tied the bag closed. With care, he untied the string and looked into the two-thirds-full bag. His heart seemed to stop for an instant. Red cornmeal!

Tears pricked his eyes. His heart throbbed with grief. It was only yesterday morning that he had left a bowl of red cornmeal at Náat's grave for his spirit to eat on its way to the house of the dead. Now, Náat had given him the food of the dead. *Is this red meal for my grave? Will my spirit soon join yours at Maski?*

The air suddenly became thick with the strange, haunting feeling. Walker closed his eyes, letting the strong sensation fill his mind.

"Do what must be done," the feeling instructed.

A shiver raced up Walker's spine, leaving his entire body shaking and cold.

"Taawa, guide me, your son," prayed Walker, as he untied and pulled off his jogging shoes. After pulling off his red Dodger T-shirt and worn blue jeans, he picked up the leggings and pulled them on. They were a bit loose, but Walker tied the throng around his waist tightly. He reached down and slipped on the moccasins. They felt light and comfortable after the sneakers.

"Náat, did your old hands make these moccasins for me to walk time in?" whispered Walker. His hand reached up and touched the eagle pendant hanging on his bare chest. A warm, peaceful feeling began to fill him. "I will do what must be done," he vowed, looking at the holy shrine.

Walker packed his shoes and clothes into the backpack. His eyes searched the floor of the cave until he saw his flashlight. He reached down and picked it up. Its beam still shone. Clicking it off, Walker placed it in the backpack next to his shoes. He slipped off his wrist watch and looked at it. It also had stopped at twelve o'clock. He slid it into the pack's small side pocket. He put the bag of cornmeal and the paho on top of his clothes. Then he closed and buckled the backpack. He picked it up, took one last cold drink from the pool and left the cave.

Sitting down next to Tag on the ledge, Walker felt Tag's eyes staring at his leggings and moccasins. Out of the corner of his eye, he saw Tag run his hands through his curly hair, shaking his head. Letting his hands fall to his side, Tag gazed down into the unknown canyon.

The minutes passed. A raven's mocking caw filled the hot, dry air.

"Okay, Walker Talayesva. You had better explain everything. Start with how and why you came to the cave," said Tag. His face was serious, but he looked ready to accept what seemed to be reality.

Walker explained that having no living parents, he had been raised by his uncle at Mishongnovi. Tears blurred his vision when he repeated his uncle's dying words. Watching Walker's face, Tag listened intently.

"So yesterday, I hitched a ride from Hopi to Flagstaff. I slept in the forest at the foot of the San Francisco Peaks last night. I caught another ride here this morning. I was just returning the prayer stick to the shrine when the lightning hit, and you rolled into the cave."

Tag swung his legs slowly in the air. His eyes scrutinized the canyon below him. After about five minutes of silence, he turned to face Walker. "Well, Walker, you've walked time and I've just tagged along." The giant grin spread across his freckled face. "At least we are living up to our names. Boy, would my Dad be envious. I sure hope I get to see him again to tell him all about it."

"I hope you do, too, but I'm not sure what we're going to find down there. I have a feeling it's going to be dangerous. Maybe you should stay in the cave until I . . ."

"No way, buddy," Tag said, standing up and brushing the dust off his blue jeans. "I'll just keep tagging along with you. Excuse the pun."

Walker laughed and stood up. "Well, whatever we find down there, one thing is for sure; the ancient ones won't have pizza on every fire pit."

"Well, I guess it's up to us to teach them how to make it."

Walker answered, "I wish it were going to be that easy."

# 5

Walker's palms started to sweat as he watched Tag climb down the sheer face of the cliff. Tag was awkwardly balancing his long body as he lowered his right foot, trying to locate the next toehold. The tip of his left sneaker was wedged into a small crevice. His fingers clung to mere cracks in the limestone.

"It sure was easier climbing up to the cave than this climbing down," Tag shouted to Walker, who was standing a good seven feet below him on the trail. "It seemed like the toe and finger grooves were dee—" Tag's left shoe slipped out of its narrow footing. As he slid downward, his left knee scraped along the rugged rocks. His fingers fought to maintain their hold. His feet frantically felt for support. The toe of his right sneaker slid into a narrow crack, stopping his fall. He pressed his thin body into the cliff's face.

"Were deeper," Tag finished his sentence into the rock. Taking a breath, he looked down at Walker. "It just goes to shows how much erosion can take place in seven hundred years."

Walker swallowed the fear in his throat. Grinning up at Tag, he cupped his hands around his mouth and called, "It just shows that you bahanas have feet too big for your own good." His heart thumped as he watched Tag climb the rest of the way down.

"Are you sure you still want to come with me?" asked Walker, seeing Tag wipe the sweat from his freckled face.

"Anything is better than climbing up that cliff again," answered Tag, looking up toward the cave. Turning to meet Walker's eyes, he smiled. "Besides, after seven hundred years, I'm starved. Let's go see what the Sinagua are having for lunch."

Walker led the way back down the narrow path toward the main trail. The air was hot, dry, still. Except for the muffled sound of Walker's moccasins and the dull thudding sound of Tag's sneakers hitting the ground, the canyon was quiet.

*Náat, I have walked time, but not alone,* Walker thought. He chuckled, thinking about the noisy bahana following him. He wondered how this city boy would like sleeping on the hard ground, not having flushable toilets, and eating who knows what? Tag thought the Hopi Reservation was primitive! Walker shook his head. Yet as Náat would say, "He has a good heart and deep courage."

A high-pitched shriek shattered the quiet air, echoing off the canyon walls. Walker stopped. The hair on his neck was standing on end, his scalp tightening. He could feel Tag's fear in the air between them.

Just as the echoing died, a second cry filled with fear pierced his ears, "Taawa . . ."

"This way," called Walker over his shoulder, bounding down the trail. "It's coming from farther down."

Walker heard Tag exclaim, "Never a dull minute around here."

Walker sprinted down the path, scanning the area around and below the trail, trying to locate the sound. The echo had died; the canyon air was still. He saw the fork in the trail ahead, and his feet slowed. His mind questioned. Which way? Up toward the cliff dwellings or down deeper in the canyon?

In answer, the strange, haunting feeling filled his mind. "Down, down," it prompted with an almost overpowering intensity.

Walker started down the chosen path. He turned his head to look back at Tag. The bahana's big feet were kicking up rocks and dust, half-running, half-tripping down the steep trail.

"Great Taawa, have pity on this noisy bahana . . . protect him," prayed Walker.

The path was getting steeper now, leading down and around a deep limestone overhang. Walker's moccasins slipped. He skidded to a stop at the outside edge of the path. Catching his breath, Walker looked down over the ledge and saw the winding trail below.

A thin, petite girl with blue-black hair flowing almost to her waist stood frozen on the path below. Her slim arms crossed her chest. Her eyes were squeezed closed. Her lips formed a straight, tight line of fear across her oval-shaped face. Yet Walker could hear the soft rhythmic humming sound of an old familiar prayer song. A rattling sound accompanied the girl's soft humming, sending a cold shiver racing up Walker's backbone. In the middle of the trail, coiled just a few inches from the girl's sandaled feet, was a huge rattlesnake.

Looking down at the snake poised to strike, Walker's heart thundered in his throat. A cold shudder shook his body like an earthquake. His palms were as wet as if he had just washed them.

Yet in the same instant, the distinctive rattling sound, accompanied by the rhythmic humming, flooded Walker's mind with vivid memories, unforgettable sounds, and keenly sharp images.

Walker's ears seemed to fill with the beat of cottonwood drums, gourd rattles shaking, and deep, throaty singing. In his mind's eye, Walker again experienced the annual Hopi Snake Dance at his village.

He saw a long, double line of Hopi Snake Priests dancing almost side by side in the village plaza. Each dancer was dressed in a knee-length, dark brown, leather kilt with a black snake painted around the bottom. Thick, white, woven sashes were tied around the priests' waists. From the back of each sash hung a red fox pelt. The priests' bare chests were painted reddish-brown and were hung heavy with turquoise jewelry. White eagle feathers tied in their long, black hair fluttered in the air. With each of the dancers' steps, Walker heard the unforgettable clacking sound of the tortoise shell rattles tied to the back of each dancer's right knee.

Walker narrowed his mental picture to a single pair of dancers in the snakelike line. The priests' faces were painted brown with white lightning flashes down their cheeks. A cold shiver shook Walker's body as he visualized a live rattlesnake held firmly but gently in the mouth of one of the dancers. The poisonous snake was held just below its flat head, with its eyes flattened against the priest's painted cheek.

Walker tried to focus his memory on the snake priest's partner, the teaser. The teaser danced slightly behind and to the right of the priest holding the snake. The teaser's left arm came around the other dancer's right shoulder holding him tightly. In the teaser's right hand was a carved branch about a foot long. White-tipped eagle feathers were tied to the end of it. Holding the snake whip close to the snake's head, the teaser stroked, distracted, and mesmerized the snake with the movement of the sacred eagle feathers. Walker knew that only the teaser's harmonious thoughts and skill with the whip kept both dancers from being bitten by the deadly snake.

Hearing Tag's heavy footsteps, Walker's mind snapped back to the present. He turned to see the bahana running down the trail toward him. In one swift motion, he moved away from the ledge and put his index finger to his lips.

Tag's mouth closed before any sound could escape. His big feet stopped short, jerking his tall body forward.

With his right index finger still against his lips, Walker motioned with his left hand for him to come. With short, quick steps, Tag moved up next to him. He pointed over the trail's edge to the girl below.

Tag's face grew pale. He whispered, "What are we going to do?"

"How good a shot are you with a rock?" asked Walker, sliding his backpack off, opening it.

"You have got to be kidding!" Tag exclaimed, turning to look at Walker.

Walker pulled out the prayer stick and started to unwrap it. "Once we get close enough, I'll use the paho to distract the . . ."

"Hey, wait just a minute," interrupted Tag, in a harsh whisper. His eyes were like bowling balls. "I've heard about how you Hopis dance with live rattlesnakes in your mouths as a religious thing. But remember, I'm just a dumb white kid!"

"The eagle is the snake's mortal enemy; its feathers have special power over it." Walker laid the paho on the ground at his feet. He buckled the backpack closed. "Once the snake is mesmerized by the movement of the feathers, you just smash it with a rock," Walker instructed. Then flashing a grin, he added, "A big one, please."

He put his backpack on, picked up the paho in his right hand and started down the trail. He could hear Tag mumbling, "'Just smash it with a rock,' he says."

A minute later, he heard Tag huffing behind him on the trail. Walker glanced back over his shoulder. The bahana was lugging a football-sized rock.

The trail went around a large boulder, then turned sharply down toward where the girl stood. Walker stopped on the trail about ten feet above the girl to wait for the bahana.

Tag's breath was coming in short gulps. He stopped next to Walker. "Are you sure this is going to work?" he whispered in between breaths.

"Think good thoughts, happy thoughts; Taawa will guide you," answered Walker. "Move very slowly and quietly. Try to stay just behind me."

With the paho in his outstretched right hand, Walker stepped toward the coiled snake. The snake's threatening rattle thundered in the air as he moved closer.

Walker's mind raced, trying to recall every detail of how the teasers moved and twisted the snake whip to make the feathers flutter and dance. In all the years he had watched the sacred ritual, had he ever seen a priest bitten by a snake?

He now could see the beady eyes in the snake's black-masked face. Its coiled, olive-yellow body was covered with leopardlike black designs. Six rattles shook on its black-tipped tail.

"Great Taawa, forgive your son for using the holy paho to kill my brother the snake," prayed Walker, moving closer. "Guide my hand . . . and the friendly bahana's, too."

The girl's humming seemed to echo Walker's silent prayer. Her eyes were still closed tight. She seemed unaware of him.

Walker could hear Tag moving right behind him. Holding the paho out before him, he crouched down, almost kneeling forward. He started to move the prayer stick back and forth. Its eagle feathers fluttered gently in the hot air. With each cautious step, Walker twisted, turned, and swayed the paho. An age-old song rose within him. In deep, throaty tones, he sang the sacred words that had been sung for hundreds of years by the Hopi Snake Priests as they sought rain for their crops.

Walker's eyes focused on the coils just a foot or so before him. The snake's masked head bolted around to face him, its blind eyes seared toward him. The snake's forked tongue darted in and out, licking the scents in the air. The eagle feathers danced. The snake's eyes jerked from Walker's face to the paho. Its head followed the dancing movement of its enemy's feathers as it came closer and closer, inch by inch.

# 6

Walker's heart hammered against his chest. Only the sacred words of the ancient prayer song that he sang prevented total fear from invading his body and soul. As he twisted and turned the paho in his shaking hand, the eagle feathers danced with a simple grace, luring the rattlesnake's complete attention.

Walker felt Tag's quick movement beside him. The football-sized rock came smashing down toward the snake. The ancient song died in Walker's throat as the snake's head was crushed.

"Taawa, thank you," Walker prayed silently. He looked up at the girl. Staring down at the dead snake, her almond-shaped, black eyes were wide with astonished confusion.

She was about Walker's age. Her beautiful oval face was thin with full lips and high cheek bones. Straight bangs hung just above her dark, expressive eyebrows. Her waist-length, blue-black hair glistened in the bright sunshine. She wore a short shirt of yellow handwoven cloth. Draped over her right shoulder was a loose-fitting yellow mantle that came down to the top of her skirt. She wore a thin, white shell bracelet around her left wrist. A strand of very small turquoise beads hung around her graceful neck.

Watching the girl's lovely but terrified face staring down at the snake, Walker stood upright. The girl's eyes flashed up from the snake into his eyes. The haunting feeling washed over Walker in a huge wave. His head felt dizzy, out of focus. There seemed to be no air in his lungs.

The girl's eyes filled with a new type of fear. She bolted down the trail. Walker gulped for air and started after her before she could get far.

"Sewa—little sister," Walker said in Hopi, reaching out touching her shoulder. "We come in peace."

The girl stopped. She turned, looking up into Walker's eyes. Again the mysterious feeling came over Walker. Deep inside he knew that in some way, this beautiful young girl was a part of the reason he had walked time.

"Thank you for killing the snake," she said, looking down at her sandals. Her voice was quiet yet strong, with a musical quality to it. Her words were strange but very Hopi sounding. Yet deep in his mind the language was familiar; Walker could understand what she was saying.

Without looking up she asked, "Who are you people?"

Walker smiled. "Hopi."

"Hopi?" asked the girl, bringing up her eyes.

"Yes. It means People of Peace. We live on the tall mesas northeast of the sacred mountain." Walker found himself somehow speaking the words in the girl's own language.

The girl nodded, again lowering her eyes.

"Hey, Walker, what did she say?" Tag asked. It had

taken him a minute or two to pull himself back together after smashing the snake.

At the sound of Tag's voice, the girl jerked her head up. Walker realized that she was seeing the bahana for the first time. Her eyes widened as she looked at his freckled face. A smile crept across her lips. She stared at Tag's curly, wild hair. A giggle escaped her mouth. She quickly covered her mouth with her hand and lowered her eyes.

"Is he Hopi, too?"

"No. Tag is bahana, white. He is a friend. He is the one who smashed the snake," Walker said, nodding at Tag.

Moving down next to Walker, Tag asked, "What did she say?"

"She said thank you for killing the snake," Walker replied, still looking at the girl.

"Nothing to it, just like you said," stated Tag, grinning down at the pretty girl next to him. "Who is she? How can you understand her?"

"Her language is almost like Hopi." Walker was glad that Tag hadn't asked how he knew how to speak this strange yet familiar language. He didn't know himself.

Walker asked, "What are you called?"

The girl looked up. "Len'-mah-nah."

The hair on the back of Walker's neck prickled. He felt the blood drain out of his face. He looked back at the snake. "Her name is Flute Maiden," Walker managed to say.

At the strained sound of Walker's voice, Tag turned to him. "Are you okay? You look a bit shaky all of a sudden."

"I'm okay. It is just that the Flute Maidens are the holy ones that . . . that . . . They are deeply involved with the snake dance. They—Oh, I'll explain it all later." Walker felt

43

flustered, almost angry. He wished the bahana would quit asking questions. Turning to Flute Maiden, he said, "I'm Walker, and this is Tag."

Flute Maiden nodded. Her face became serious, her voice low. "The men are guarding the trails into the canyon. They are not letting any traders or people from other places in. How did you get here?"

"We came by lightning," answered Walker.

He saw Flute Maiden's eyes grow large again. She stared back at the dead snake. She looked back at Walker. Her eyes fell upon the eagle pendant hanging on his bare chest. She drew in her breath, biting her bottom lip. Her searching eyes quickly dropped to Walker's feet.

What was she looking at? wondered Walker. Feeling uncomfortable, he shifted his weight from one foot to the other. Was she staring at his moccasins or maybe the red birthmark on his right ankle? He shifted his feet again.

Flute Maiden gazed back into Walker's eyes. A gentle smile played on her lips. She nodded her head slightly. "You must be very careful," she said in almost a whisper. "Times are dangerous, very dangerous for our people. That is why no one but our own are allowed in the canyon. Come, we cannot stay here. It is not safe." Flute Maiden turned, and hurried down the trail.

"Come on, Tag. She says it's dangerous here," Walker said, starting after her.

"Dangerous? What could be more dangerous than rattlesnakes?" Tag asked, his hands on his hips. He looked at the snake, then at the two hurrying down the trail. Waving his hand, he called, "Hey, wait for me. By the way, did she say what was for lunch?"

Within fifty feet, Flute Maiden left the trail and went into a thin clump of weathered pine trees. Dry pine needles fell on Walker as he pushed through the boughs. On the other side of the trees, Walker could see that they were on another path of some kind. Flute Maiden moved quickly over the rocks and around the sage and cacti in her way. But Walker had to watch his footing. They were climbing upward again. By the general direction they were taking, he knew that they must be doubling back toward the cliff dwellings.

"Where in the heck are we going?" asked Tag. His foot slipped on a rock. It went rolling down the side of the canyon. "They must have better trails than this to get to the ruins—I mean their homes."

"This must be a back entrance of some kind. I don't think many people go this way." Walker said, looking back at Tag.

"I can see why!"

"Shhh," hissed Flute Maiden as she stopped and turned toward them, shaking her head. Looking at Tag's big grin, she shrugged her shoulders. She scrambled up and over a limestone ledge and disappeared.

Wiping the sweat off his forehead, Tag whispered, "Just like a mountain goat."

"Naw—she just doesn't have big feet like you bahanas. Come on, let's go before we get lost," Walker said, starting to climb up the steep ledge.

"Get lost! We are zapped back in time, seven hundred and umpteen years, and he's worried about getting lost."

# 7

Reaching the top of the ledge, Walker saw Flute Maiden standing at the base of a deep limestone overhang. She motioned for him to hurry. Behind him, he could hear Tag muttering something about getting lost.

When he reached Flute Maiden, Walker saw a single mud-and-rock dwelling built under the limestone overhang. Without speaking, Flute Maiden slipped into the narrow doorway. Walker wiped the sweat off his forehead as he waited for Tag. For having such long legs, he sure did not move very fast, thought Walker. Seeing Tag almost trip, he realized that Tag was not really slow, just clumsy. Walker chuckled. Around all these steep cliffs, though, just being clumsy could be very dangerous.

"I've never seen this ruin—I mean house before," Tag exclaimed, catching up with Walker. "I know I would re-member it since it is out here all alone. Most ruins—I mean houses—were built in small clusters. This one must not have survived all the years," Tag said, bending almost in half to follow Walker through the low door.

When Walker's eyes adjusted to the semidarkness, he could see that the room was very small, only about five feet by three feet. The air was cool and dry.

"Walker, this ruin doesn't smell like the rest of the ruins—it doesn't smell lived in or even old," Tag said, moving in next to Walker.

"It's a storage room." Walker pointed with his chin, "Look."

Brownware jars of different sizes were lined up against the back wall. The largest jars were about three feet tall and a good yard wide in the middle. The smallest jars were about ten inches high and a few inches wide. Large one- to three-foot-tall, plain yucca baskets lined the other walls.

"I bet this room probably didn't even survive the very earliest pot hunters," said Tag, his eyes wide. "This is a pot hunter's grandest dream come true. Do you know how much just one of those jars or baskets would be worth on the black market today—I mean back in the future?"

"Shh," answered Walker, sitting down on the dirt floor. His eyes followed Flute Maiden, who was searching among the baskets. She pulled out something, looked at it, shook her head, and returned it to the basket. She started to rummage through another basket.

Easing himself down next to Walker, Tag asked, "What's she doing?"

Walker didn't answer. The haunting feeling suddenly whirlwinded around him. He closed his eyes, letting the feeling sweep through his body. A vague image swirled around and started to take form in his mind.

The figure of a petite woman bending over one of the tallest baskets emerged in his mind. Her long, black hair was pulled back at the nape of her neck and hung almost to her hips. Straight, long bangs covered her high forehead. Her skirt, a soft reddish skin with small, white shells sewn around the bottom hem, came well above her knees. Two strands of tiny white shells wrapped around her slim neck. A loop of matching shells hung from her pierced ears.

The mysterious feeling pumped through Walker's entire body. In his mind's eye, he saw the strangely familiar woman stand up from one of the baskets with something in her hand. She turned toward Walker. Her kind, black eyes twinkled; her full lips smiled. Her voice was soft and loving. "Ahh, here it is . . ."

"Walker, Walker," Tag's loud voice shattered the vivid images in Walker's mind. "Hey, what's the matter? Flute Maiden is talking to you."

Walker's eyes flew open. Flute Maiden stood before him, holding a small piece of brown buckskin in one hand and a pair of sandals in the other. "Are you all right?" she asked. Her voice was like a soft breeze.

Walker swallowed hard and managed a nod. He felt dizzy. His mind was cloudy. His heart was beating like a ceremonial drum.

Flute Maiden looked relieved. She pointed her chin toward Tag, "It is too dangerous. His clothes will cause too many questions. I found him some sandals." She held up the yucca sandals. They were like the ones she was wearing. "And a covering." Smiling, she held up the small piece of buckskin.

"What is she saying?" Tag asked in a suspicious tone.

Walker stifled the laugh building up in his chest. Here was Tag's first real challenge. "She said she found you something to wear."

"You have got to be kidding—that little piece of nothing!" Tag exclaimed, glaring at the buckskin Flute Maiden held out toward him.

Flute Maiden motioned for Tag to stand up.

"Look, Tag, for some reason things are dangerous here for strangers and right now you'd look mighty strange to the ancient ones," Walker said. "So hurry and get your clothes off."

Tag began to protest, but the look of urgency in Flute Maiden's eyes stopped him. He stood up. With a scowl, he started to pull off his T-shirt. "Okay, but I'm keeping my underwear on under that—that thing."

Walker chuckled, watching Tag pull off his shoes and stockings. Flute Maiden gathered them up. He could tell that she was examining them as she walked to the back of the room. He wondered what she thought of the red striped tube socks, hot pink T-shirt, and the huge shoes with the long, florescent-green shoelaces. She quickly fingered each item one more time. Then without a word, she rolled the shoes and socks in the T-shirt and hid them behind a large brown jar.

"I can't believe I'm doing this," Tag said, pulling off his blue jeans. "Maybe I should have stayed in the cave."

Flute Maiden took the blue jeans out of Tag's trembling hands. She picked up the buckskin, knelt down, and started to wrap the skin around Tag's skinny waist.

Walker held his breath to keep from laughing out loud. Tag's freckles were washed in a deep scarlet blush. Flute

Maiden's nimble fingers wrapped, tucked, and folded the skin into a neat loin cloth that covered Tag's brightly colored underwear.

Flute Maiden stood up. Turning Tag around, she inspected her work. "It's a bit big for him, but it will do." With a mischievous smile, she folded up his blue jeans. "He has lizard legs."

Laughter thundered in Walker's chest and echoed off the close walls. Flute Maiden giggled, holding out the pair of sandals to Tag.

"All right, what did she say?" Tag snorted, with his hands on his waist.

Trying to sound serious, Walker answered, "She said to put the sandals on."

"Hey! These are made out of yucca cactus," Tag said, eagerly taking the sandals. "Archaeologists found pieces of them in the ruins. They're on display in the Visitor Center—or they will be back in the future. But no one ever found a complete sandal. In fact, they just guessed that the pieces they found were sandals." Tag put his big foot down on the mat of tightly plaited yucca leaves. "They could be just a bit bigger, but not bad." He tied the braided strap of yucca fibers over his foot and around his ankle. "Not quite Nikes, but a lot lighter and cooler." Tag held up his foot to show Walker. A grin spread across his face. "My Dad would just about die to have a pair of these. Thank you," he said to Flute Maiden, who was hiding his blue jeans with the rest of his clothes.

Taking his backpack off, Walker opened it. Laying the bag of red cornmeal and the paho on the ground, he pulled out his watch and clothes. He fingered his metal flashlight for a moment, thinking. If for any reason they needed to escape at night, the rugged canyon would be treacherous without light. Giving it a squeeze, Walker set the flashlight by the cornmeal. He rolled his watch up in his clothes and handed them to Flute Maiden. "We had better hide these, too." While she hid them, Walker replaced the cornmeal, paho, and the flashlight in his pack. Standing up, he slipped it on his back.

"We have to go now, before the men come back to the village. We must get to my father, Great Owl, before anyone sees you," Flute Maiden said, starting to move out of the door.

Walker followed. "Great Owl?" he whispered, the haunting feeling creeping slowly back into his mind.

"He is a Seer, who sees and understands all things. He's the only one who can protect you now," stated Flute Maiden. "Stay close."

"Are we going up to the cliff dwellings now?" Tag asked, trying to adjust his eyes to the bright sun again.

Walker started after Flute Maiden up a very steep, narrow path. "She is taking us to Great Owl."

Following close behind Walker, Tag asked, "Who's he?"

"Flute Maiden's father. He'll protect us."

"Protect us from what?"

The air was filled with ear-shattering shrieks and yelps as five men with long spears appeared ahead of them on the path. Four more armed men sprang from among the rocks behind them. With sharp spearheads thrust forward, the men quickly surrounded the three climbers.

# 8

S top!" ordered the leader of the group. He looked about eighteen or nineteen years old but was only Walker's height. His dark brown skin pulled tight across his powerful chest and shoulders. His short, leather loincloth showed very muscular legs and thighs. His long, black hair was pulled away from his foxlike face. Straight bangs hung over his small, slanted eyes.

He stalked toward Flute Maiden. With a hard shove, he pushed her against the rocks at the inside of the path. Before Walker could move more than a step toward her, the young man's spearhead was thrust up against his chest, just below the eagle pendant. He felt the sharp point all but cutting into his skin. The young man's deep-set eyes glared at the eagle pendant.

"Why are you sneaking into our canyon on the skirts of a girl?" the young man snarled, pushing his spear point into Walker's skin.

Walker felt the point prick his chest. He stared into the cold, black eyes. Never had he seen such hatred, bitterness, and contempt in one's eyes before.

"I cling to no one's skirt. Nor do I hurt harmless women," Walker stated in a low but steady voice. His heart was hammering in his chest, but he stood tall against the spear, his eyes locked with its carrier.

"Who are you?" the young man shrieked. His shrill voice echoed off the canyon walls.

Walker felt drops of warmth ooze down his chest as the spear point was thrust deeper into his skin. Still he stared into the hostile eyes without flinching. The putrid smell of death filled his nose and lungs. *If I am to die, then I will die as a man,* Walker thought. "One that knows better than to scream his wants to the sparrows and mice," Walker answered.

The man's eyes glared with anger. With a deep growl, he curled his thin lips back, showing his brown, rotting teeth.

"He is right, Gray Wolf. You sound like a naughty child howling demands—demands that you have no authority to make." The firm, authoritative voice came from behind Flute Maiden.

Without lowering his spear, Gray Wolf swung his head around to the direction of the voice. Walker followed his gaze.

On the path above Flute Maiden was a second group of armed men. The man who had spoken was taking long, confident strides toward them. He was about the same age as Gray Wolf and about the same height. He, too, looked underfed yet strong. He wore a short, red loincloth. His blue-black, shoulder-length hair was tied in the back. He wore the same straight bangs above his eyes as the others. Tension showed in his handsome, round face. His intelligent, black eyes were large, his nose broad, his back straight and strong.

"White Badger," fumed Gray Wolf. Hatred seemed to boil in his eyes as they met White Badger's for an instant. Walker heard him growl again.

The men lowered their spears, letting White Badger pass. Taking Flute Maiden's arm, he helped her up. "Sister, are you all right?"

Flute Maiden nodded her head. She whispered something to him, nodding toward Walker and Tag. With long, powerful strides, White Badger stalked down to them, his eyes never leaving Gray Wolf. With a quick, powerful jerk, he wrenched the spear away from Walker's chest, out of Gray Wolf's hand, and hurled it to the ground.

"You have no right to harm my sister," White Badger said in a low voice. His intense eyes were locked with Gray Wolf's. "And you have no authority to question these visitors. Only the Warrior Chief has such authority when the High Chief is gone. Or maybe you have forgotten that it was I who was chosen Warrior Chief, not you."

Gray Wolf lashed back, "I have every right to stop strangers who are here to steal our food and bring the spirit sickness." His voice was as sharp as a knife.

White Badger's face was tense, but his voice was even. "If they were here to steal our food, why would they save Flute Maiden from a rattlesnake?"

Walker saw Gray Wolf's eyes widen, then blink. "So these—these boys just appeared even though all trails and entrances into the canyon were closely guarded. How did they get here? Through the air? And they can control rattlesnakes!" Gray Wolf was looking around at the other men in the group, trying to gain their support. "What more do we need to know! They are two hearted—witches! Witches here to spread more sickness and pain. Witches that have come to steal our very spirits away!"

Walker heard mumbling around him. He could see fear and confusion in the faces of the men surrounding them. Some took steps backward, others lifted their spears toward them.

"I say kill these witches right now! Cut out their double hearts and burn them before any more hunger and death come to our people!" Gray Wolf's high-pitched voice screeched.

"A child has more logic than you," said White Badger staring at Gray Wolf. With firmness, he spoke just loud enough for all to hear. "Why would witches save Flute Maiden from the rattlesnake? Witches would have let the snake bite her, just so they could enjoy watching her die in agony. No, these strangers are not witches. They are just very courageous."

Turning his back on Gray Wolf, White Badger looked around at the frightened men. Meeting each man's eyes, he continued with a firm voice. "As the Warrior Chief in command, I say we take them to Great Owl. Only he can—"

"Take them to your father?" Gray Wolf interrupted with scorn. "His eyes and heart will be blinded because of Flute Maiden. He is just an old man ready to die like our chief," he ranted, throwing up one arm and shaking his fist.

The men shifted from one foot to the other, whispering to each other. Fear filled the air.

"No," stated a man to the left of Walker. He was about

twenty-five years old and had a long, deep scar running down his right cheek. "Great Owl is a Seer. He will know if they are witches. He has always held the good of the people in his heart; his eyes have always seen truth for our people. If there is danger here, he will see it. Let's take them to Great Owl now!"

Walker's heart pounded in his throat. He glanced at the men surrounding him. They talked to each other in low voices for a few seconds, then heads began to nod.

"Yes, let's take them to the Seer!"

"The Seer will know what they are."

"We must take them to Great Owl now!"

Walker looked at Gray Wolf. His face was twisted with disgust and hatred. With a growl, he swung around and stomped to where two of his men stood together.

"Come quickly before Gray Wolf changes their minds," White Badger whispered to Walker.

Walker nodded. "Thank you, friend."

"You saved my sister's life. It is I who owe thanks." White Badger looked deep into Walker's eyes. He continued in a low voice. "We must go before any more can be said against you. We have waited a long time and time is running out."

With brisk strides, White Badger started up the path. Flute Maiden smiled and nodded at Walker and Tag, then followed behind White Badger. In silence the other men lined up in single file and began climbing the steep, rocky path.

Gray Wolf glared at Walker, growled, then fell in line. But just before he started up the path, he turned to stare at Walker. An ugly smile curled his thin lips.

Walker waited until Gray Wolf was well up the path before he looked at Tag. "Are you okay?"

Tag nodded. His freckles stood out on his pale face. "Boy, I thought we were goners for sure. What is going on?"

"I'll explain as we walk. You're doing great. Just keep doing what you're doing."

Tag screwed up his freckles in confusion. "What am I doing?"

"Keeping quiet!" whispered Walker. He started up the path to the ancient ones' village and possible death.

# 9

Being accustomed to climbing the rugged terrain of the canyon, White Badger and the others moved with remarkable speed and agility. Lagging behind, Walker and Tag followed with less ease and grace.

"Why did Gray Wolf accuse us of being witches?" asked Tag, his worried voice audible to only Walker.

Walker wiped the sweat out of his eyes. He turned his head so the warm breeze carried his words back to Tag. "For some reason we are . . ." Walker reached up to touch the eagle pendant hanging on his chest. "That is, I am a threat to Gray Wolf. He wanted to kill me the minute he saw my pendant. But he couldn't in front of the others, not without a good reason. So he gave them an excellent one, hoping they would kill us."

"Wonderful! What happens if this Great Owl person decides we are witches?" Tag sputtered, trying to keep up with Walker.

Walker took a deep breath and let it out. He had been studying that, along with other questions. Why did the name of Great Owl summon the mysterious, haunting feeling? Why did it have a strangely familiar sound to it? Walker shook his head in confusion. "Flute Maiden said Great Owl is a Seer. True Seers can peer into one's heart, into one's very being. If Flute Maiden is correct, then her father will see us for what we are."

Tag slipped on a loose rock and caught himself. Shaking his head, he asked, "Do you think he will see my empty stomach?"

Twenty feet ahead Walker saw an enormous, fifty-foot cliff rising straight up. White Badger strode to the limestone wall, then disappeared into the cliff's face. Directly behind him, Flute Maiden also vanished into the cliff, as did each man after her.

Walker moved quickly up the path, straining to see. Gray Wolf stood at the head of the line. He turned to stare at Walker. Pulling his lips back into a snarl, he turned and disappeared into the base of the cliff.

"Neat trick. Too bad he can't just disappear for good," Tag stated.

Walker stepped up behind the last man in line. He could see the spot where the people seemed to be melting into the cliff. A *passageway*, thought Walker, watching the next man slip behind a huge, flat slab of limestone leaning against the bottom of the cliff. The slab was about twenty feet long. Rising about twelve feet into the air, its top rested against the cliff's face. Walker's mind took in every detail of the slab's location, realizing that the passageway could also serve as an escape route.

Walker felt Tag's breath on his neck. The bahana looked over his shoulder and watched the next two men slip into the passageway. Walker turned his head to look at Tag. He could tell from the expression on Tag's face that he was thinking the same thing.

"Come," said the man with the deep scar running down his cheek. They were the last ones on the path. From the tone of his voice and the caution in his large, black eyes, Walker knew that Scar Cheek was still uncertain if they were witches or not. Yet he had had the courage to walk just ahead of them, Walker realized. His opposition to Gray Wolf had taken great inner strength. Such a man would be a good friend to have, Walker noted.

Walker nodded at Scar Cheek. The man turned sideways and stepped into the narrow opening between the rock slab and the base of the cliff. Walker followed, with Tag right behind him.

"I guess they don't have to worry about any fat enemies getting up this way," Tag mumbled. "If this gets any narrower, I won't have any skin left on my back or my nose. There's got to be an easier way up to the ruins—I mean to their village."

"I am sure there is. But this is probably the fastest way up to Great Owl," Walker whispered. *And to our deaths?*

About five feet into the passageway, Scar Cheek stopped, pointing upward. Walker saw a path of chiseled notches leading up the side of the cliff and ending just below the top of the slab. At that point, a deep crevice in the limestone began and continued up to the top of the cliff. Using the grooved path of toeholds, Scar Cheek scaled the rock to the crevice. Looking down at Walker, he swung his thin body into the crevice and disappeared.

Walker slipped the toe of his moccasin in the first notch and lifted himself up. He heard Tag mumble, "Mountain goats. You have to be a mountain goat to live here!"

Walker could tell by the depth of the notches that much time and effort had been spent chiseling them out. Climbing up to the crevice wasn't difficult using the deeply grooved notches.

When Walker reached the last notch, his head was about four inches below the top of the limestone slab, his back rubbing against it. He stretched his head around the edge of the crevice and looked up. The natural shaft was about six feet deep and three feet wide. Forty-five feet above him, Walker saw the bottom of Scar Cheek's feet climb over the top edge of the cliff.

He looked down at Tag. "You okay?"

Tag nodded. "Pretty ingenious, I have to admit. Great defensive planning, to say the least," he added, pulling himself up to the second set of toeholds.

"Wait till you see what comes next," Walker exclaimed, swinging his body into the crevice. On the left side of the crevice, notches had again been chiseled out of the limestone. Walker realized that the crevice was so deep and narrow that it would be almost impossible for anyone on the ground to see him climbing up.

Even with the deep toeholds, scaling up the sheer cliff took all of Walker's strength and concentration. Hot air blasted into the crevice. Sweat ran down his body in little streams. He heard a raven's mocking cry as he carefully inched upward. Resting, he turned his head to look out of the limestone ravine. The cloudless, blue sky seemed harsh. The canyon's cliffs were hostile.

"Great Taawa, guide us, your sons, in this time of long

ago. Help us to find harmony with the people of this canyon. Guide our minds and hearts," Walker prayed, starting up the cliff again. "And our feet."

He heard Tag following below. "I can't believe I'm doing this!"

Looking up, Walker could see the top of the crevice. Scar Cheek's square face appeared over the edge, staring down at him. Walker felt the hair on his neck stand on end. As Walker lifted himself up onto the last toehold, Scar Cheek's hand reached down toward him.

*If he lets go,* Walker's mind raced, *the ancient ones won't have to worry about any witches.* He looked up into the black eyes above him. They were filled with apprehension toward a stranger as well as concern for another human being. Walker had seen this same look hundreds of times in the eyes of his Hopi people.

Stretching up, Walker grasped Scar Cheek's broad hand. With amazing strength, Scar Cheek lifted Walker up and over the edge of the crevice.

Scrambling to his feet, Walker said, "Brother, thank you."

Scar Cheek nodded, turned, and crouched down, reaching over the edge again. Tag came flopping out of the crevice like a fish being hauled onto shore. His sweaty face was flushed. He sat panting on the dusty ground. He smiled up at Scar Cheek. "Walker, please tell him thank you for me," Tag said, struggling to his feet.

"Vaava, kwa kwa," Walker told Scar Cheek.

Scar Cheek grunted, turned, and started up another narrow path among clumps of dry beeweed, yucca cactus, and boulders. Walker turned to Tag. Shrugging his shoulders, he said, "Come on."

Within minutes, Walker heard noisy excitement. The sounds of nervous men explaining, worried women questioning, and anxious children whinnying reminded him of his Hopi village. He had heard this same kind of commotion each time something dangerous or strange had occurred in his village.

A small, dark face with jackrabbit eyes peered out at him from behind a boulder. Another round face with curious eyes under a curtain of long, straight bangs peeked out from the other side of the boulder. Walker winked at them. The frightened faces disappeared.

The path curved around a large outcrop of limestone. Walker saw a group of women huddled together at the entrance of a cliff dwelling. They were dressed in skirts and mantles similar to the ones Flute Maiden wore. One woman clutched a wooden cradle board with a tiny, sleeping infant strapped inside. Two small, identical, naked children hid behind the legs of the pretty woman in the center. Their thin faces peeked around their mother's legs. The last woman held a large, white, ceramic water jug on her hip. The women stopped whispering to each other, lowering their eyes to the ground. Walking past them, Walker felt fear in the air.

The face of a young girl appeared at the entrance of the next rock house. "Come away from the door. They are witches!" exclaimed a harsh voice from within. The girl's curious face vanished.

Gray Wolf had wasted no time in spreading the word about witches. Of course, such news would always travel like the wind, thought Walker. They passed three more clusters of rock dwellings, each with women and children around them. Walker realized that he had not seen any men. Were they all with Great Owl? *Waiting for us!* Walker thought, with fear tightening his stomach. He turned to look at Tag.

Tag's eyes were like bowling balls gawking at the ancient ones. Walker frowned and shook his head. "It is rude even for a witch to stare so hard," he whispered in a firm voice.

A man with a long, yellow cape that came down to his knees rushed out of a dwelling. With a lopsided limp, he hurried up to Scar Cheek. The man's words came in quick, excited spurts. "Scar Cheek, the others are at the meeting place." he exclaimed. His dark eyes darted back at Walker and Tag. "You must hurry. Gray Wolf is trying to . . ."

Scar Cheek touched the man's shoulder and mumbled something to him. With a nod, the man limped down the path in the opposite direction and disappeared into a dwelling.

Turning to Walker, Scar Cheek stated, "We must hurry." He started up a path wedged between two cliff dwellings.

"Why do I feel as if I am about to be put on trial?" Tag asked, following close on Walker's heels.

The hair on Walker's scalp tightened as a shiver raced up his back. "Because you are."

# 10

The rocky path wound up to the top of the long lime-stone overhang under which some of the homes were built. Then it traversed the overhang for two hundred yards. It climbed again at a very steep grade till it reached the rim of the canyon. Here the path ended at a narrow, limestone bridge with sheer drop-offs on each side. The well-worn limestone spanned a good five feet to a broad ridge extending out from the canyon's rim.

"The fort! They're taking us to one of the forts!" exclaimed Tag upon reaching the natural bridge. "The forts were built on top of wide, flat promontories like big islands that jutted out from the rim. There were five in all, each built directly above a different group of ruins—I mean homes," stated Tag, sounding like a tour guide. Walker stopped to listen. "Grave robbers and pot hunters had pretty well destroyed the areas before any real studies could be done. Dad said no one was sure what the forts had been used for." Pointing to the steep cliffs surrounding the ridge in front of them, Tag continued. "Since there is only one way into and out of each island, the forts could have been built for protection. Or they could have been used for ceremonial purposes. They are—or they were—in restricted areas, so the tourist couldn't get to them. But my Dad took me to one once. I'm not sure if this is the same one or not. It all looks so different."

"Shh," hissed Scar Cheek from the other side of the short bridge where he stood waiting for them. He motioned for them to hurry.

"All right, all right, we're coming," Tag answered with a perturbed sound to his voice.

Walker realized that Tag still did not understand the gravity of the situation. How could he? All his life he had lived in an advanced, complex society with an intricate legal system that guaranteed liberty and justice to all. Walker's hands were wet. His stomach twisted in knots. *Here,* he thought, taking a deep breath to calm his thundering heart, *one person can have the power of life or death.*

Crossing over the limestone bridge, Walker saw an eight-foot-tall rock wall. Guarding the only entrance into the wall were two of Gray Wolf's men. Walking toward them, he felt their eyes glaring at him, and as he passed by them, the smell of death filled his nose.

As Walker stepped inside the entrance, the haunting feeling shot through him, and he swayed slightly. He stopped short, every nerve in his body taut. Blinking his eyes, he tried to focus on what he saw.

The high, thick wall followed the contour of the triangular-shaped island. Ten rock dwellings were built along the inside of the protective wall. They were small shelters with no windows and unusually low, narrow

T-shaped doors. Walker realized that they were not used for daily living.

In the middle of the enclosed island, about fifty armed men sat on the ground. They were in four neat rows with their backs toward the entrance. All faced a stagelike platform made of rocks mortared with mud. It was about three feet high, five feet deep, and ten feet long.

The breath caught in Walker's throat. He felt his eyes widen. A stone shrine stood in the center of the platform. It was almost identical to the shrines found in the Hopi's sacred underground ceremonial rooms called kivas.

The ancient ones' shrine stood about three and half feet off the ground. Its limestone slabs had been skillfully cut and mortared together to form a perfect two-foot-by-two-foot square with a flat top. A steplike shelf ran along the bottom of the shrine. Brightly colored prayer sticks adorned the shelf. Offerings made to what gods? wondered Walker.

At his next thought, a cold shiver ran through Walker's body. Was there a small hole dug into the top of the platform about six inches from the base of the shrine? Walker's mind raced; his heart hammered. Such a hole, which the Hopi called a "sipápu," would mean that the ancient ones believed in the same creation story as the Hopi—a story that told how all peoples of the world had emerged into this world from just such a sipápu at the bottom of the Grand Canyon. How many other beliefs and traditions did these ancient people share with his people? Walker wondered, forcing his eyes to leave the stone shrine.

Gray Wolf stood on the right side of the shrine, his legs firmly planted. His arms were folded across his chest. His thin lips were pulled across his sharp teeth in a snarl.

White Badger stood on the left side of the rock shrine.

Walker could see tension in his body, but his strong face was controlled. His eyes moved over the crowd of men. He seemed to be making eye contact with each man as if to determine those that would follow him or be swayed by Gray Wolf.

Walker felt all eyes on him as he followed Scar Cheek, who was threading his way through the seated men. He tried to keep his back tall, his shoulders squared, his eyes aimed at Scar Cheek's long, black hair. His heart pounded in his throat; the sound echoed in his ears.

*Great Taawa guide my thoughts, my words . . .* Walker prayed.

He heard murmuring rippling through the crowd. "Witches . . . Two hearted . . . Snake charmers . . . Death!" The whispering grew like a great wave, growing more intense until it echoed off the canyon walls.

Scar Cheek stopped a few feet from the platform but motioned for the boys to continue. Walker advanced, Tag at his side. Stopping a foot from the base of the platform, Walker looked over at Tag. He stood tall and proud, but his freckles seemed to dance on his pale face. Small beads of sweat dotted his forehead. His fists were drawn up into tight balls. For an instant, their eyes met. In Tag's eyes, Walker saw the fear that he himself felt. He tried to smile, but his lips felt frozen.

Walker turned his head to the platform, searching the ground in front of the shrine. Six inches from the base of the shrine, he could just barely see the top of a small hole. *A sipápu!* Walker's knees felt weak.

Walker sensed Gray Wolf's eyes staring at him. He looked up to meet Gray Wolf's contemptuous yet pleased glare. If there had not been so much commotion, Walker was sure he would be able to hear him growling.

White Badger raised his spear in the air. A strained hush fell over the gathered men. White Badger's voice held authority when he spoke. "Great Owl, our Seer, has been told all concerning these strangers. Now he will see into their hearts."

Flute Maiden was climbing up the stairs on the left side of the platform. A man, stooped with age, leaned on her arm. He climbed each step one at a time. Walker could not see the man's face. He wore a tight skullcap, decorated with thousands of small, colorful beads that glistened like a rainbow. Long, thin, snow-colored hair flowed down his stooped back. He wore a brilliant red, knee-length kilt, decorated with small, white shells. A fist-sized clam shell, studded with small, square pieces of turquoise, dangled on a leather thong around his thin neck. In his gnarled left hand was a long wooden staff. Walker could see intricate designs and lines carved into the thick staff. A calendar of some sort? wondered Walker.

Without warning, the mysterious feeling raged through every cell in Walker's body. *Great Owl, Great Owl,* the words swirled in Walker's mind. His eyes clamped shut, and his throat tightened in fear. He fought through the haunting feeling to get his breath. Struggling, he opened his eyes.

Great Owl stood in front of the shrine between Gray Wolf and White Badger. Leaning on his staff, he stared down at Walker. Never before had Walker seen such eyes. They were large, soft, brown pools of light that seemed to be able to penetrate deep into one's soul—or gaze into the most distant future.

Great Owl turned his eyes toward the freckled bahana. His thin lips formed in a straight line across his deeply wrinkled face. Walker saw his eyes twinkle as he looked down at Tag's freckled face and curly hair. Walker thought he heard a soft chuckle when Great Owl's eyes stared down at Tag's skinny legs.

"Tell us what you see, old man," Gray Wolf's voice snarled.

Great Owl's strong, smooth voice answered, "I see two thirsty mouths and two very empty stomachs."

Gray Wolf lurched toward Great Owl, his fists clenched at his waist. "They are witches!"

Great Owl raised his staff at Gray Wolf, meeting his cold eyes. "I see two brave young men who risked their lives to save one of our women. I also see that they receive accusations and threats instead of welcome and thanks."

"Look deeper, old man," growled Gray Wolf. His face was twisted with anger. He jerked his body around, glaring into the crowd. Raising his spear, he screamed, "They are witches! They will destroy all of us!"

Great Owl's voice came like lightning. "I see Gray Wolf is afraid to accept the truth because the truth is not in harmony with his desire to seize power for himself."

The air was hot, quiet—thick with tension. Gray Wolf's body trembled with rage as he stared into Great Owl's stolid face. Great Owl's eyes seemed to sear into Gray Wolf's soul. Walker sensed that everyone present was holding his breath just as he was.

Gray Wolf's shoulders began to slump. His eyes broke away. With a quick turn, he jumped off the platform and stormed out through the crowd. A few men stood up and followed him out of the wall's entrance.

Tag let out a long, deep breath. Walker looked over at him. He could tell that Tag more or less understood what had just happened.

70

"What is to be done with these strangers?" someone in the gathering called.

Great Owl held up his staff. It shook in his old hand. "What should have been done in the first place; welcome and feed these young men." He lowered his arm. "They will stay at my home until our chief returns from his pilgrimage to the sacred mountain." Great Owl leaned on his staff for support. He looked tired, but his voice was strong. He gazed down into Walker's eyes. "When Lone Eagle returns, all that must be done will be done."

*Lone Eagle . . . Lone Eagle . . . death . . .* The haunting feeling swept through Walker's body. His knees swayed under him. His heart felt as if it had stopped.

# 11

The water was warm, but it soothed Walker's parched throat. He lowered the cup, made from a dried gourd. The fist-size, smooth gourd was still half full, and he was still thirsty. He knew that each precious drop of water had been carried up the steep canyon from the stream of water at the bottom. For as long as he could remember, he had hauled heavy water jugs up the high mesa to his home each day. He knew well the price paid in sweat for even such a small amount of water.

Walker passed the half-full gourd to Tag, who was sitting crossed-legged next him. In two large, noisy gulps, Tag drained the remaining water. Flute Maiden moved forward with a reddish-orange ceramic water jug and refilled the cup. With a smile, Tag guzzled down the second cup of water. Of course, Tag had never carried water any further than from the kitchen sink, Walker realized, watching the bahana drain the cup for a third time. *Here it will be different.*

Walker looked around Great Owl's mud-and-rock home. They sat a foot or so from the doorway on woven yucca mats in a semicircle facing the center of the home. The room was about fifteen feet long and eight feet deep. Even with a small cooking fire burning in the back of the room next to the limestone wall, the air was cool and dry. Smoke from the fire curled up the back wall, drifted along the rock ceiling and out the three air holes made in the stone wall above the T-shaped door.

Flute Maiden's and White Badger's older sister, Morning Flower, knelt by the smoky fire. Her intelligent eyes darted from her cooking to the men as she stirred something in a medium-sized gray pot. She was about twenty and looked a lot like Flute Maiden. Unlike her sister, Morning Flower seemed extremely shy. Walker wondered if this was because she was self-conscious about her body being swollen huge with pregnancy. Or was she just naturally withdrawn and timid? She did not live here with her father, Great Owl, but next door in her own home with her husband. Where was her husband? Walker wondered with a sudden uneasiness.

Morning Flower's young son, Small Cub, sat close to her. He was a friendly four-year-old with straight bangs and long blue-black hair that framed his quick-to-smile, square face. He wore nothing but a leather thong around his neck. A small white shell hung from the narrow thong. His large, curious, black eyes stared at them, his mouth shaped in a half-moon smile.

Walker studied the cooking area. Three fat, knee-high, plain ceramic jars of different shapes lined the back corner of the cooking pit. Each jar had a thin sheet of leather tied around its large opening. He guessed that at least one of

73

these containers stored dried corn that would be ground into cornmeal for cooking. The other jars might hold such things as pinyon nuts, acorns, walnuts, and pumpkin or squash seeds. Or perhaps they contained dried foods such as beans, prickly pear fruit, or yucca banana fruit. Walker knew that whatever was in the storage containers depended on what had been successfully grown or gathered from nature. These three jars would hold only enough food to feed Great Owl's family for a few weeks at the most. They must have other food storage nearby, Walker surmised. From all that he had seen of the canyon so far, he doubted very much that the ancient ones' storage rooms contained enough food for the coming winter.

Three white, tightly woven yucca baskets with bold black designs stood in front of the large pots. Each lidded basket was about twelve inches high and six inches around. Food seasonings such as wild mustard, dried onion, wild oregano, and salt were most likely kept in these baskets, Walker decided. The family's dishes, three neat stacks of ceramic pots, bowls, and mugs in various shades of white, gray, and reddish-orange, were placed near the baskets.

Every inch of the cooking area was utilized to its best advantage. The last bit of space against the back wall was taken up by two large, ceramic water jugs. These plain brown, five-gallon jugs were shaped like giant tortoise shells—flat on one side, rounded on the other. Each had a narrow, round opening at the top and was laced with a thick, leather shoulder strap.

In the room's opposite back corner was a stack of rolled-up mats, similar to the one Walker sat on. Even rolled up, these mats, he could tell, were longer and wider. They were probably used for sleeping on. A pile of varicolored furs was neatly stacked on the mats. Blankets? Next to the sleeping mats sat three large, yellow baskets, about two feet tall, each with a distinctive design woven into it. They had wide, open mouths. Storage for clothing and other personal items? Since Flute Maiden had placed his backpack next to these baskets, Walker felt sure that they were.

Walker's heart suddenly filled with a wave of homesickness. Great Owl's home reminded him of Náat's one-room house. Only the barest essentials had been allowed. Anything else had been stored away in the small storage area next door till it was needed. "Live with only what you need today," Náat had said many times. "It is the old way."

*How right you were, Uncle,* thought Walker, scanning the ancient ones' home.

The only sources of light in the room were the small cooking fire and sunshine through the doorway. With the mid-afternoon sun shining through the T-shaped opening, Walker could see quite well. He watched Tag glancing toward the cooking pit. Walker chuckled. The smells coming from the cooking pot were definitely not what the bahana was accustomed to.

"Flute Maiden, now that our visitors have quenched their thirst, we must see to their wounds," Great Owl said, his voice soft and warm. He sat next to Walker, his old legs crossed in front of him. His staff lay beside him.

Flute Maiden nodded, moving to the sleeping mats. Reaching into one of the large baskets, she brought out a reddish colored fur and a small, stark white, ceramic bowl. As she knelt in front of Walker, he could see that the fur was an entire pelt from a small fox. Its legs and stomach had been stitched together. Its tail was folded and sewn between its legs, making a neat little bag. Flute Maiden untied the leather thong around its neck. Reaching inside, she pulled out a small, leather pouch with a red, cotton drawstring through the top of it.

Opening the bag, Flute Maiden emptied a couple of teaspoons of fine, red powder into her hand. Placing the powder in the ceramic bowl, she poured in some water. As she swished the water around, it turned bright red. Setting the bowl down, she reached again inside her fox pouch and brought out a small piece of white cotton material.

"The skin here is just bruised," Flute Maiden said, inspecting Walker's cheek. Walker had all but forgotten striking his cheek against the wall in the cave. "The angry color will leave soon." She dipped the woven cloth into the red water and squeezed out the excess. Then she gently washed his bruised cheek with the wet cloth. The bruise was sensitive to Flute Maiden's soft touch. A strong flowery scent drifted to Walker's nose, but he couldn't match the familiar smell with a flower.

"But here," Flute Maiden continued, indicating the small cut in Walker's chest just below his eagle pendant, "where Gray Wolf's spear showed his hatred, the skin is broken. But not too deep."

The breath caught in Walker's throat. Flute Maiden's touch was gentle, but the red water stung the open wound. Whatever the red water was, it felt like iodine!

"It smells like wild geraniums," said Tag, sniffing the air. With a chuckle, he added, "Even if it doesn't kill any germs, you're going to smell great."

After rinsing the cloth again in the red water and cleaning the wound a final time, Flute Maiden reached into her fox pouch. She brought out a second leather drawstring bag. Opening this bag, she explained, "All the evil feelings have been washed out. Now we must cover the wound, so that no bad spirits can enter through it into your body." Reaching into the small bag, she brought out a clear, thick poultice on her fingers. She gently spread the ointment over Walker's wound. The stinging disappeared and was replaced with a cool, soothing sensation.

After applying the medicine, Flute Maiden's fingers stole up to touch the eagle pendant. Her serious eyes studied it.

Watching her intent face, Walker wished he could read her mind. What answers would he find there at this minute? Walker looked down at the pendant in Flute Maiden's fingers and then into her beautiful eyes. "Thank you. It feels better already."

With obvious embarrassment, Flute Maiden let her eyes fall to the ground. Gathering her things, she said, "Before you sleep tonight and again at sunrise, I must cover the opening to protect it against Gray Wolf's evil thoughts and feelings. They must not find a way into your body." She rose, taking her things with her.

"Flute Maiden is a very skilled medicine woman. Her touch is one of healing for both the body and the mind," Great Owl said with pride in his voice. "My oldest daughter, Morning Flower, has magical powers in her hands, too, but when she touches food." Great Owl nodded toward Morning Flower, who was now setting down a large gray-and-black bowl in front of Tag and Walker. It was full of something that looked like very thick stew.

Morning Flower also set down two small, gray bowls with intricate, black, wavelike designs on them. Without looking up, she moved back to the cooking area. Her son, Small Cub, who had followed her, curled himself up next to White Badger. His curious eyes stared at Walker and Tag.

Picking up one of the cup-size bowls, Walker dipped it into the serving bowl. He filled it about half full of stew. Holding the bowl with one hand close to his mouth, he put his fingers into it. Using his fingers as a spoon, he scooped up some stew and put it into his mouth. The flavor was strange but good. He could taste bits of corn, mixed with chunks of squash in the thick, spicy sauce. He dipped his fingers in the bowl again. This time he crunched into something nutty with a wild flavor to it. Acorn or maybe some kind of wild seed, thought Walker, chewing. With his next mouthful, he bit into something crisp that reminded him of bacon. It felt as if it had little legs poking the top of his mouth. Swallowing, Walker wondered how the bahana was enjoying his meal. He looked over to Tag, who had followed his example and now held a bowl of stew. He was peering down into his food with a bewildered look on his face. Walker had to stifle a laugh.

Staring up at Walker, Tag said, "My mom would just die if she ever knew that I didn't use a spoon. So maybe I'll just try drinking it." He brought the bowl up to his mouth.

Great Owl chuckled watching Tag. Flute Maiden, who had sat down on the other side of Great Owl, covered her mouth to catch the giggle that was escaping. White Badger, sitting next to Tag, watched with humorous interest. The young child burst into loud laughter. "The spotted stranger is trying to . . ."

"Hush, Small Cub," whispered White Badger, gently pulling his nephew to him.

Lowering his bowl, Tag muttered, "It's so thick it won't

78

even run out." He smiled weakly. "Oh well, my mom will never know, right?" He dipped his fingers into the bowl. With a quick jerk, he put them into his mouth. As he chewed, the expression on his face changed from apprehension to approval. He took another finger scoop. "Mmmm," he mumbled, nodding his head and chewing. Suddenly his mouth froze. His eyes grew wide with a look of shock and disbelief. He jerked his head around to face Walker. Three tiny, thread-thin legs dangled out of the corner of his mouth.

Walker grinned. Scooping more stew into his own mouth, he watched the bahana.

Tag looked back into his bowl. He shrugged his shoulders and swallowed hard. "Not exactly chicken noodle soup, is it?" he mumbled. Staring at the rest of his stew, he shrugged his shoulders again, took a deep breath, and dipped his fingers back into his food.

Finishing his stew, Walker set the bowl down. After licking his fingers, he said, "Morning Flower does have magic with food."

There was still stew left in the large serving bowl. Walker's stomach was only half full, but he knew that this food would be needed to feed the others.

Tag also set his bowl down without helping himself to another serving. "Best grasshopper, or whatever, stew I've ever eaten," he said, smiling at the others. He winked at Small Cub, sending a giggle through the little boy.

Morning Flower came from the cooking area carrying two small, white, ceramic drinking mugs. One was covered with a complicated black design of swirls and lines. The other had a simple outline of an owl painted on it. Keeping her eyes cast toward the ground, she handed each boy a mug.

"Thank you," Walker said, taking the mug with the

owl. A strong, minty scent drifted up from the warm tea. The mint tea filled Walker's stomach, satisfying his remaining hunger. Putting his mug down, he said, "Great Owl, thank you for your kindness. My stomach is full."

Great Owl nodded his head. Looking deep into Walker's eyes with his large penetrating ones, he said, "Tell me about your people, Walker of Time."

A shiver slithered up Walker's back. Did Great Owl know that they had traveled back in time? Of course. He was a Seer. This realization gave Walker an unsettled feeling in the pit of his stomach. Taking a deep breath and letting it out slowly, he began. "My people are the Hopi, the People of Peace. I am of the Water Clan. My village, Mishongnovi, is northeast of the Holy Peaks, many days' journey from here," Walker told Great Owl. He knew the others were listening intently. "My people also live in homes made of rock and mud, but they are built on top of great cliffs. We are farmers like your people, depending on mother corn to feed and sustain us."

"Do your people have lots of corn to eat?" interrupted Small Cub, with hunger in his voice.

"Hush," whispered White Badger, this time setting his nephew in his lap. Small Club looked up into White Badger's serious face. White Badger pinched his lips together in displeasure. Small Cub squirmed around on White Badger's lap. Finding a comfortable spot, he sat still, with his eyes on Walker.

"If my people have lived in harmony with Mother Earth and each other and if our prayers have been said in the proper way, yes, we have enough corn, squash, and beans to eat. But many times our stomachs have growled with the anger of hunger," Walker said, looking at the thin boy. He could almost count Small Cub's ribs.

Great Owl's old head nodded, his lips in a slight smile across his wrinkled face. His thoughts seemed to be far away, but his eyes remained on Walker. After a long silence he asked, "And your friend, his people?"

Walker looked over to Tag, who was just wiping his mouth after finishing his tea. Walker chewed on his lower lip in thought. After a minute, he answered, "Tag's people, the bahanas, are different from both our people. Their ways are strange. Some are good, some not so good . . ."

"What do the speckled bahanas eat?" asked Small Cub, his large eyes peering at Tag.

White Badger's hand came down gently onto Small Cub's shoulder, "Shhh . . ."

Walker laughed. "Tag, Small Cub wants to know what bahanas eat."

With a twinkle in his eye, Tag said, "Tell him we eat ice snow, painted all the colors of the rainbow. The very best kind is chocolate." Tag smacked his lips.

"I don't think Small Cub has ever tasted chocolate," Walker said.

"Oh, you're right," Tag said. "Sort of mind boggling trying to keep the two time periods straight. Let's see. It tastes like . . . like wild raspberries. I know they have those here." Tag grinned at Small Cub.

Walker translated. Small Cub's large eyes filled with wonder while the adult faces reflected amazement mixed with uncertainty.

Great Owl asked, "Where are the bahana people now?"

Walker had to think. Where were the bahanas in A.D. 1250 or thereabouts? "Now, they live very far away to the east over the great mountains, across the vast flat lands, and beyond the great waters. Someday they will cross the great waters to come to this land."

"Many, many moons till they come . . ." Great Owl's voice sounded distant. His eyes seemed to peer into the future. "Our people will no longer live in the walls of this canyon . . ."

The mysterious feeling swept over Walker, almost stopping his breath. His head swam. The sound of his heart thundered in his ears. Black spots began to blur his vision, till everything around him faded into darkness.

Yet in this total darkness, he began to see a steep, narrow path winding its way up and through the limestone cliffs. The call of an eagle rang in the air as it circled high above the trail. A line of people climbed the path . . . Men carrying spears and bows, with huge baskets slung over their shoulders . . . Women with small infants in cradle boards bound to their backs and young children clinging to their hands . . . Older children following their parents, stopping often to look back toward their abandoned homes in the cliffs . . .

# 12

Walker, Walker!" Tag's voice penetrated and echoed in Walker's mind, shattering the darkness with its vision.

Blinking his eyes, Walker's mind came back to the present. Tag was shaking his shoulder, with a look of fear on his face.

Walker glanced around at the others. Each person, even Small Cub, sat erect, quiet, intensely watching him. Great Owl's old hands gripped his staff, his gnarled knuckles white, his eyes seeing deep inside Walker's mind. His white-haired head nodded. A sigh escaped his thin chest. He closed his eyes as in prayer.

The cavelike home was as quiet as a tomb. To Walker, the air had become thick, hot, stifling. His head throbbed with pain. His hands and face were wet with sweat. He tried to swallow the hollow, washed-out feeling that was caught in his throat. Bringing his hands up, he pressed his fingers to his forehead, trying to push out the pounding pain.

"Yes, the time draws near, Walker of Time," Great Owl said, opening his eyes and looking toward Walker. Seeing his distress, Great Owl spoke quietly to Flute Maiden. She rose and brought Walker a cup of water.

Taking small, even swallows, Walker felt the tightness leave his throat. Drawing a deep breath, he set the cup down, keeping his eyes on it. He did not want to look into anyone else's face, not till he could gather his thoughts together.

"You have come far, my son," Great Owl's voice was warm and smooth, "very far, very fast. You and your friend must be at peace. Nothing more can be done until our chief, Lone Eagle, returns. You will be safe with us till then." His face was washed with a deep weariness mixed with fatigue. "This old man must rest now."

Walker got to his feet. Pain throbbed in his head with every movement. He turned to the doorway. Bending down, he placed his palms on the hand ledges on each side of the door and went outside.

The sun's afternoon rays were bright. It took a few seconds for Walker's eyes to focus. He took one deep breath after another, letting each out slowly through his mouth.

He walked to the edge of the narrow path that ran in front of Great Owl's home. The scent of smoke from cooking pits filled his nose. The noise of daily life drifted in the air. The familiar sound of corn being ground came from somewhere down the path. The echoes of children's hungry voices seemed to surround him. From within nearby dwellings, he could hear the hushed, worried voices of adults. The pain in his head began to fade. He felt a hand on his shoulder.

"Are you okay?" Tag asked. "What happened in there? You sort of blacked out or something. But your eyes were wide open. You looked as if you were seeing something."

Turning to face Tag, Walker shook his head. "I'm not sure what happened. I did see something, but I don't . . ." his voice trailed off. His eyes fell to the ground.

Tag pressed, "What did you see?"

Shrugging his shoulders, Walker answered, "I'm not sure, or at least I don't understand what I saw." Walker paused, staring down into the canyon. He let the sights, smells, and sounds drift around and through him. They were all so familiar. "Have you ever walked into a building or a room for the first time and had the feeling that you had been there before? Even when you knew you hadn't?"

Tag nodded. "It's called déjà vu. I guess everyone has felt that way at one time or another."

"But felt it so strongly that it almost overwhelms them?" Walker bent down to pick up a small rock. Squeezing it in his right hand, he said, "I'm not sure what's happening here or why we are here. But something deep inside tells me," Walker tossed the rock into the air and caught it with his other hand, "it's not just to teach the ancient ones to make pizza. I am also sure," Walker said, looking toward Great Owl's home, "that they know why we are here."

"Then why don't we just go back in there and ask them why in the heck we were zapped back here?" Tag demanded.

With a smile, Walker tossed the rock toward Tag. As Tag caught it, Walker stated, "It is not the Hopi way. Or these people's way to ask questions that will be answered in their own time and place."

"You mean we are just going to wait around till who knows what happens to us?" Tag tossed the rock back to Walker.

Catching it in one hand, Walker answered, "Yes. More or less. Except while we wait, we are going to keep our eyes and our minds open. My Uncle used to tell me, 'Answers to questions are all around you if you are willing to see them.' I think we should learn as much as we can about these people before their chief comes back."

"You mean mix with the natives?" Tag's face broke into his toothy grin. "Great idea! There's a ton of things that I need to see. Most of their culture, their very way of life, was lost in time, so I need to . . ." Tag stopped, putting his hands on his thin hips. "Okay, what's so funny?"

Walker laughed, shaking his head. "You! Back in the future you said that you were sick of hearing your father talk about dead Indians all the time. Now you can hardly wait to start doing living archaeology."

Smiling sheepishly, Tag shrugged his shoulders. "Well, I guess I have some of my Dad in me. Do you realize what we are seeing, hearing, and touching? We are with an ancient civilization that literally just disappeared off the face of the earth, leaving very little behind. People centuries from now are going to examine, study, and wonder about what we are actually living right now!"

Hearing noise behind them, they turned toward the houses. With some difficulty, Morning Flower crawled out of Great Owl's low door. Flute Maiden followed close behind with a water jug slung over each shoulder. Small Cub scrambled out behind her. The two women talked in soft voices for a minute. Then Morning Flower entered the T-shaped door of the dwelling next to Great Owl's.

86

"Time to learn the first and most basic aspect of daily life here," Walker said, nodding his head toward Flute Maiden. Walking up to Flute Maiden, he took a jug from her shoulder. "Bahanas are expert water carriers," he said, passing the jug to Tag. Tag took the jug and began to examine it with great interest. Walker chuckled. He took the other jug from Flute Maiden and put it on his own shoulder.

"I want to go, too! I want to go, too!" cried Small Cub, tugging at Flute Maiden's hand.

Smiling down at her nephew, Flute Maiden answered, "You may go, but you must carry your own water jug. Run get it."

While they waited for Small Cub, Walker studied the houses. There were two other small dwellings also built under the limestone overhang. They were nestled under the low, tapering edges, one on each side of the main houses. Walker was almost sure that these low, compact rooms were used for food storage. How full were these rooms? wondered Walker.

"Do all bahanas have such . . . such . . . ," Flute Maiden asked Walker, twirling her hand around her head.

"You mean curly hair. No. He's just lucky," Walker answered with a chuckle, staring at Tag's wild mass of curls.

"Hey, you two are talking about me again, aren't you?" Tag demanded.

"What could we possibly say?" Walker answered, flashing a smile at Tag.

Small Cub reappeared carrying a small water jug slung over his thin shoulder. Flute Maiden started down the path. Walker followed behind her, with Tag next. Small Cub trotted close on Tag's heels, watching every movement the bahana made.

The trail was well worn and narrow. It wrapped around in front of another limestone overhang that housed seven or eight dwellings of various sizes. Clusters of women and small children gathered around the homes. The women were talking, but their voices quieted when they saw the group approaching. Only the eyes of the children continued to watch them as Flute Maiden stopped at the first home.

"Gray Dove," said Flute Maiden in a soft voice to a middle-aged woman sitting in the doorway. "How is your mother's cough today?"

Gray Dove looked up from the piece of leather that she was scraping with a sharp stone knife. Her black hair was streaked with gray, yet her pretty face was youthful. Only her eyes looked tired and old. The stone knife trembled in her hand as she spoke. "The tea you left helps calm the cough." There was gratefulness in her voice, but it had a cautious undertone to it.

Flute Maiden nodded. "Gray Dove, these are our visitors, Walker and Tag." Turning to Walker, she continued, "Gray Dove is well known for her great skill with leather. People from all over bring their uncured skins and hides to her. She makes very beautiful moccasins, clothes, bags, and other items from them. To wear or own one of Gray Dove's creations is an honor."

Gray Dove's face shown with pride, but her eyes remained on her work.

At the adjoining home, two women, obviously a mother and daughter, sat on yucca mats working with wet, gray clay. Nearby, three newly formed bowls and pots were drying in the sun on a flat limestone slab. A sleeping infant lay strapped in a cradle board near the younger woman. After asking the women about their families, Flute Maiden once again introduced Walker and Tag.

The oldest woman, whose shoulders were hunched forward a bit, looked up at Walker. Her small, deep-set eyes studied his face for a minute, then fell upon Walker's turquoise pendant. Her thin lips parted in a smile. "Welcome." Her voice was thin yet held warmth.

Walker saw a look of surprise in the daughter's face at hearing her mother's words. She was about sixteen years old with a pretty but anxious-looking face. Her graceful fingers were shaping a long, snakelike coil of clay. She wrapped and pinched the coil into a vase-shaped pot, her eyes never leaving her creation.

Tag knelt down in front of the young woman. "That's going to be a beautiful pot when you are finished," he said, watching her every movement.

At the sound of the strange words, the young woman's face filled with fear. Her fingers stopped. Her hands trembled.

"My friend says your pot is very beautiful," Walker interpreted, kneeling next to Tag.

Small Cub plopped down by Tag. "Fawn makes the best pots in all of our village. She made my drinking mug," he said with pride.

The fear left Fawn's face. Her lips turned up, but her eyes were still riveted to the wet clay she molded. They sat watching her skillful fingers shape her vase. Walker realized she was using the same coiling technique that he had seen Hopi potters use. With one last pinch, Fawn turned the wet clay around in her hands, inspecting its graceful lines. She picked up a piece of dried gourd that lay by her hip. With careful, gentle strokes, she started to smooth the coiled sides of the vase with the piece of gourd. Walker knew that it would take her a long time to smooth and even out the walls of the vase using this primitive tool. It would take her even longer to polish the vase's entire surface with the small, flat river stone that lay in her lap, ready to use. Walker's scalp tingled. How many times had he seen these same kinds of crude tools, which had been handed down from generation to generation, used by Hopi women to create their beautiful pottery?

At each door in the cluster of homes, the same scene was repeated. Flute Maiden inquired about the health of the family, then introduced Walker and Tag. Walker could see fear mixed with suspicion in each face. Yet Flute Maiden had a way of easing this with her words. She was well liked and respected by these women. Walker sensed that she was enlisting the women's trust, along with their support for what lay ahead.

Tag's friendly smile and Small Cub's obvious admiration toward him helped win over the children. By the second home, Tag was holding Small Cub's little, dark hand in his large, freckled one.

At each house they witnessed living archaeology. They watched one woman sewing tiny shells onto a kilt with a thin bone needle. At another home, a very young girl was learning to make corn cakes from her very old grandmother. Tag sat enthralled, watching a middle-aged woman skillfully plaiting yucca leaves into sandals. At the last house in the group, a mother was teaching her small children the words of a song while she worked on weaving a large basket. Her voice was strong and clear, her fingers skillful and fast. The basket, made from long strips of yucca, grew before their eyes.

About fifty feet down the path, they came to another group of homes nestled under a cliff. Again at each house, Walker and Tag were introduced and fears were calmed while they watched the village women at their daily work.

At the last home, a woman stood at a large, waist-high boulder just outside her door. She held a mano, a smooth grinding stone, in her hands. With long, even strokes she moved the mano back and forth on the top of the boulder. Walker could see a well-worn trough in the boulder's surface where the corn was being ground into fine cornmeal.

Flute Maiden stopped. "Littlest Star, how is your baby today?"

The petite woman looked up from her work. Her large, expressive eyes spoke of great worry. "She is asleep now. Her older sister sits with her. She still can't hold food very long." The woman shook her head, wiping her brow. "She grows as thin as a blade of grass."

"I will come back to see her after I get water," Flute Maiden promised, reaching out to touch the woman's thin shoulder. "There is a very strong tea made from the dried stems of a special plant that grows only on the Sacred Mountain. I think it is time that we try it. I will bring some for her."

Littlest Star nodded. "Thank you." Her eyes stole a glance at Walker, then returned to Flute Maiden with a questioning look. Her hand tightened on the mano, turning her knuckles white.

Flute Maiden said, "Walker and Tag have come in peace. They are our friends."

Littlest Star raised her eyes to glance at the strangers. Her eyes met Walker's for an instant and held. Lowering her gaze back to her grinding rock, she nodded and started back to work.

"Littlest Star's husband is Scar Cheek," Flute Maiden said, as they moved on down the trail. "They are good people. People you can trust."

"You know," Tag told Walker, "that very boulder she is using as a metate or grinding stone is still there. I mean in the future. It's right on the paved trail that the tourists take. I must have passed it a thousand times. I never really thought about someone actually using it!" Tag smiled. "She's lucky to have a metate just outside her door, and it's one that she can even stand at. You have to kneel down to grind on most metates," Tag explained. "All that kneeling must be murder on your back, not to mention your knees." Bobbing his head up and down, he concluded, "Someone was real smart to start using that boulder as a metate."

Walker thought of the small grinding room at his village. Four deeply troughed metates sat on the hard dirt floor. They were placed in two rows facing each other so that the women could visit while they worked. No one had spoken to him as he had ground the red corn for Náat's grave. A wave of grief washed over him. Tears clouded his eyes. Tag was right. Kneeling to grind the red corn had been painful to his knees and back, almost as painful as it had been to his heart.

At the very last home in the village, Flute Maiden knelt down beside an old woman sitting in front her doorway. The woman's white hair was tied into a bun at the base of her thin neck. Her face was a sea of wrinkles from which two small eyes peered. Walker could see a cloud of film over each eye. Her wrinkled hands were busy weaving long strips of yucca fibers into a mat. Her eyes stared straight forward.

Flute Maiden knelt down beside the woman. "Singing Woman, it's Flute Maiden," she said, hugging the blind woman. The old woman smiled, patting Flute Maiden's hand. Flute Maiden looked down at the half-finished mat. "I've never seen such a beautiful design in a mat before."

"Neither have I," the old woman said with a merry chuckle, "but I like the feel of it on my fingertips."

Pushing his way forward, Small Cub knelt beside Singing Woman. "I'm here, too," he said. "We brought the strangers with us. One of them is speckled like a bird's egg and his hair is all . . ."

"Hush," the old woman scolded, reaching for Small Cub, hugging him to her. "You are too old for such rudeness. They are our guests." Then in a loud whisper, she teased, "I wish I could see the speckled one's hair that flies in circles every which way."

Small Cub squealed in delight. Walker and Flute Maiden exchanged glances, looked at Tag, and began to laugh.

Tag put his hands on his hips, pursed his lips together, and shook his head. "What I would give to understand what you are saying about me," he grumbled. Then looking down at the warmth in Singing Woman's face, he shrugged his shoulders and grinned.

"Tell me, Small Cub, does the other one wear something around his neck?" asked the old woman with a sly smile. She was still hugging the boy in her lap.

Small Cub's eyes stared at Walker's pendant. "Yes."

Singing Woman's voice took on almost a musical quality. "It is a seashell cut into the shape of our brother the eagle, covered with small, even chips of turquoise."

Small Cub looked up into the Singing Woman's face. "How did you know? You can't see with your eyes."

"I see with my heart." Peering in Walker's direction, Singing Woman said, "Welcome." She lifted her hand toward him. He knelt down in front of the woman and took the thin, bony hand into his. It was cold and felt as fragile as dry leaves. Yet as she held his hand, he felt great strength radiating from her. The mysterious feeling swirled in the air around Walker.

"My waiting is over. Time grows short for this old one. For you," she squeezed Walker's hand tightly, tears filling her sightless eyes, "it just begins. My son, let your heart always see as well as your eyes. Peace and strength go with you and your people, Walker of Time."

# 13

In silence, Walker followed Flute Maiden down the steep trail that worked its way to the floor of the canyon. He was trying to piece together all that had happened in the last hours. From Flute Maiden's stillness, he knew that her mind also weighed heavy.

Small Cub's chatter filled the air. He held Tag's hand, stopping every few minutes to point out things: a bird, a lizard, or an unusual rock formation. Even though Tag couldn't understand a thing Small Cub was saying, he grinned, nodded his head, and added to Small Cub's comments. "You are right. That's a three-toed woodpecker . . . Wow! That's the biggest hooded lizard that I've seen in seven hundred years . . ."

Listening to those two, you would think they understood every word the other one said, thought Walker. *Maybe they are listening with their hearts.*

After a good ten minutes' descent, the path evened out onto the narrow floor of the canyon. Walker could see a dry streambed stretching down the middle of the canyon. From the lack of any kind of foliage, except for a few stunted cacti, Walker knew that the stream had been dry for two or three years at least.

Heading west, Flute Maiden followed a rocky path along the streambed. As the canyon widened, there were small, cleared patches of ground along the dry bed. They ranged in size from three to ten feet square. Walker had worked with Náat on such plots of ground near his own village. He knew that these spots had once been small gardens for corn or squash. Water from the stream would have been hauled in jugs to each plant. Rainfall and natural run-off during the monsoon weather would have supplied additional moisture. Each small spot could grow five to ten plants. Compared to the bahanas' huge farm fields of the future, Walker realized, these gardens were minute. Yet with special care and prayers, a few plants could yield a surprising amount of food. He also knew from his own farming experiences that it would take many of these small gardens to feed the people he had met in just the past hour. He remembered the hunger in Small Cub's voice. His uneasiness began to grow.

Walker left the path, taking the few steps that led to one of the larger growing areas. Kneeling down, he scraped away the top layer of dusty soil. He scooped up a handful of the second layer of dirt. Walker let the parched soil trickle through his fingers. He looked up at Flute Maiden, waiting on the path. She had a hauntingly familiar look in her eyes. Walker had seen this same worry many times in the eyes of his people when the rains didn't fall and the crops died.

Tag squatted down beside him, followed by Small Cub. Tag questioned, "What is it?"

"It was a garden. Guessing by the size of it, I think it was a corn field that had maybe ten or twelve plants at the most."

"You mean like the small patches of corn that your people grow on the sides of hills and at the foot of the mesas?" Tag asked. He picked up some soil. Small Cub dug his fingers into the dirt.

Walker nodded. "These people are dry farmers, too. In order to survive, they have to plant every useable piece of earth and use every available drop of moisture. In the last few minutes, we have passed ten areas like this one." Walker turned to look at Tag. "All of them have been abandoned for a couple of years at least."

"So the stream must have been dry that long?" Tag asked.

"Longer. They probably still planted here even after the stream dried up, hauling water to each plant and hoping for the monsoon rains to come. I am sure that they needed to keep these areas growing and did. Until . . ."

"Until it became impossible to keep them alive because of the lack of water," Tag finished. He shook his head and stood up. Small Cub popped up beside him.

Walker rose, brushing his hands off. "Flute Maiden is waiting for us."

They followed the streambed for another ten minutes before they came to an area that was planted with corn. The wilted, brown stalks were only knee high. Walker could see only one small ear of corn on each of the ten or so plants.

They passed three more small gardens, all promising little or no harvest. Walker wondered where the men who worked these areas were. As if Flute Maiden had read his mind, she said, "Some of the younger boys grow corn here. The men farm the fields on top of the canyon's rim."

How big were those fields? wondered Walker, following Flute Maiden. If there wasn't enough moisture to sustain crops here in the canyon, how could there be enough on the rim of the canyon? Walker's uneasiness knotted up in his stomach. *How can these people survive?* he asked himself.

Within minutes Walker smelled water. A small stream seemed to appear out of nowhere. The clear water bubbled up out of the ground between giant boulders at the foot of a deep ravine that ran to the top of the canyon. The ancient ones had dammed up the area, making a shallow pool about three feet by five feet wide. There was not even a trickle of overflow to wet the wide, dry streambed that continued to wander down the canyon. How much longer could this small spring support all the people? wondered Walker, staring at what seemed to be the only useable water source.

Three women with water jugs sat by the pool talking. They appeared to be between sixteen and nineteen years old. All were dressed similarly to Flute Maiden. A small, bare baby sat playing near one of the women.

"Running Boy, Gray Rabbit, Little Cloud!" Small Cub called to a group of small, naked boys playing on the nearby boulders. "Come! Come see! I have brought the speckled stranger!" Small Cub scrambled past the others, running ahead to his friends.

Flute Maiden led the way to the edge of the pool. She spoke to each woman by name. In turn, she introduced them to Walker and Tag. Walker saw fear in all the women's faces.

By this time Small Cub and his friends had surrounded Tag, with Small Cub chattering like a magpie. "Come with us," Small Cub cried, pulling on Tag's hand and pointing to where the boys had been playing in the boulders. His friends stood a few steps away. Their eyes were wide with wonder staring at Tag.

"Okay, okay," said Tag, nodding his head. He took the water jug off his shoulder and handed it to Walker. "I have to admit that it's sort of fun being the center of this kind of attention." He grinned, taking Small Cub's hand. "Let's go." Small Cub led Tag away and the other boys cautiously followed a few steps behind.

"Be careful," called one of the women; worry flashed across her face.

"Tag will watch over them, Bright Star," said Flute Maiden. "How is your husband's leg?"

Still watching her son, Bright Star answered, "Better, since he is using the medicine you gave him." Seeing that her son was safe, she smiled at Flute Maiden. "Thanks to you, it is almost healed. He is even working in the fields now."

Walker moved a few feet away from the women. Kneeling down, he began filling the water jugs while listening to the women chat. Within minutes, the tension in the air had lifted. Again Flute Maiden had set the fearful minds at ease.

Taking the last jug out of the water, Walker set it down beside him. He sat back and watched Flute Maiden as she visited with the others. Her face seemed to shine with an inner serenity and harmony. Her movements were fluid, graceful, and self-assured. The strange but now familiar feeling reached its fingers into Walker's mind, but this time with a soothing touch. He felt that he had known this beautiful ancient girl all of his life. He was at ease with her ways and thoughts. He closed his eyes, letting the feeling calm his mind and heart.

A harsh voice shattered the quiet moment. "So, again I find you with helpless women and children."

Walker's newly found inner harmony crumpled. Throwing open his eyes, he saw Gray Wolf and three of his men standing a few feet away. Gray Wolf's fingers were white as he clutched his long spear shaft. Waves of hatred rolled off him. Walker rose to his feet, never letting his eyes leave Gray Wolf's twisted face.

"Of course, women's and children's spirits are the easiest to steal," Gray Wolf snarled, taking menacing steps forward, "or are you using your witchcraft to poison our water?"

Walker heard frightened gasps and whispers from the women behind him. His heart hammered in his chest.

"Maybe you should try stealing my spirit," snarled Gray Wolf, springing at Walker. He smashed the butt of the spear shaft into Walker's ribs, knocking him into the pool.

Anger, along with the natural instinct to fight, blazed in Walker even before he landed backward in the cold water. The rocks he landed on were hard. In an instant, he was back on his feet standing in the ankle-deep water. Gray Wolf stood poised with his spear, waiting for Walker to counterattack.

*Waiting to kill you,* the realization crashed through Walker's anger into his logic, *to kill you in self-defense.* With water running down his tense back, Walker clenched his fist and his teeth. He squared his shoulders. Looking straight into Gray Wolf's hate-filled eyes, he stated loud enough for all to hear, "I have come in peace, and in peace I will remain here."

A startled cry shattered the hot air. "My baby, my baby!"

Turning, Walker saw Bright Star cradling her toddler. The child's face was a bluish color. Its eyes were closed.

"She was just playing with a rock, but now she's not breathing!" screamed Bright Star, shaking the limp child. "She's not breathing!"

"The witch!" screeched Gray Wolf, lifting his spear toward Walker. "The witch has stolen the child's spirit!"

# 14

Walker and Flute Maiden reached the mother, who was holding the limp child, at the same time. "The rocks—she must have swallowed one of the rocks," Flute Maiden said, reaching for the child.

"Give her to me," Walker said. In one quick movement he took the child from the mother's arm and turned her around so that her back was against his chest, her head and shoulder slumping forward. Just below the baby's tiny rib cage, Walker pressed his finger tips with a jerking motion. Nothing happened. He repeated the squeezing motion a bit more firmly. A marble-sized rock popped out of the child's mouth and fell to the ground.

Walker could hear the child's mother crying, the frightened women murmuring, and Gray Wolf screaming words about witchcraft and death.

Walker quickly turned the baby around in his arms. Her small face was bluish-gray; no breath lifted her tiny chest. "She's still not breathing on her own," Walker cried, feeling panic rise in his chest.

From out of nowhere, Tag appeared. His large hands took the tiny, lifeless child in his arms. Kneeling down, he laid the baby on her back. Putting his fingers into the small mouth, he opened it and tilted the head back. He lowered his mouth over the baby's mouth and nose and blew air in. He raised his head, listened for a few seconds, then puffed again into the blue lips.

A small cough escaped through the baby's mouth, then a small gasp for air, and then another. In seconds, the baby's color was returning, her chest lifting and falling on its own. The tiny, black eyes opened. Seeing Tag, the baby started to whimper, then howl.

"It's okay, little one," Tag said, lifting the baby off the ground. Bright Star, tears streaming down her worried face, eagerly took her daughter into her arms.

One of Gray Wolf's men moved up next to Bright Star and put his arm around her. His face was distorted with both worry and relief. He reached out to touch his daughter's tiny hand as she cried. Walker could see tears in the man's eyes. The man looked at Tag. "Thank you," he mumbled.

Bright Star, still cradling the baby, sat down on a nearby rock, trying to soothe her crying. Her husband followed her, kneeling down in front of her, softly talking to the baby.

Walker looked at Flute Maiden. Her eyes were shining with tears, but her face held a look of pride. She nodded her head and smiled.

"Very clever, very clever," growled Gray Wolf, who was standing a few feet from them. "Stealing the baby's spirit, then blowing it back." He laughed deep within his chest. "Witches, the both of you. Now we have the proof!" He spun around and started up the path with one of his men following.

Gray Wolf's third man stood watching Bright Star and her family. Confusion and bewilderment twisted his face. His intense eyes moved from Walker to Tag and then darted back to the baby who was now eating at her mother's breast. He shook his head in uncertainty but made no move to follow Gray Wolf.

"Let's get the water jugs and get back up to Great Owl's," Walker whispered to Tag, "before Gray Wolf comes back with a lynch mob." His heart was still thundering against his chest. His stomach felt as if it were tied into a double knot. The feeling of relief for the baby was overpowered by fear and doubts. What would he have done if Gray Wolf had continued his attack? Could he have defended himself against him? True, he had been a champion on the school's wrestling team, but he knew it wasn't a friendly wrestling match that Gray Wolf wanted. What chance would he have against a spear or a stone knife? Remembering the red cornmeal, the food of the dead, that Náat had put in his backpack, a shiver raced up Walker's spine. He felt sure now that it had been sent for his grave.

•   ◆   •

The sun's rays were beginning to fade by the time they had climbed back up the long, steep trail to Great Owl's home. Leading the group, Walker saw Great Owl sitting on a mat outside his home. He sat facing the setting sun, his eyes closed in prayer. At the sound of Small Cub's chatter, the black eyes opened. His head turned toward them.

104

"Grandfather, Grandfather," cried Small Cub, running ahead of the others. "Bright Star's baby's spirit escaped! Tag caught it and blew it back into the baby!"

Walker saw Great Owl's eyes widen slightly. "Small Cub, your mother needs the water in your jug. Please take it to her," Great Owl said.

"But Tag . . ." Small Cub started, but seeing the stern look in his grandfather's face, he nodded. Without another word, he climbed through the door of his home.

Tag was huffing and puffing when he reached Great Owl. He wiped the sweat off his dusty forehead. "What a climb, not to mention carrying this heavy jug full of water," he groaned, taking the jug from his sagging shoulder. Holding the jug in his arms, he flopped down on the ground and leaned back against the stone wall of Great Owl's home.

A smile spread across Great Owl's wrinkled face as he looked at the tired, panting bahana with his long, white, freckled legs sprawled out in front of him. His eyes peered at Tag. His smile became a tight line across his face. What is Great Owl seeing? wondered Walker, watching the two. Could Great Owl see Tag going back to his parents? Or was he seeing Tag's life coming to an end here? Walker's scalp tingled. He didn't want to know what lay ahead for Tag or himself.

"Here, Tag, I'll take the jug in," Walker said, taking the jug out of Tag's arms. He followed Flute Maiden into the house.

Walker found Great Owl still intently studying Tag's face when he returned. Tag still leaned against the house. His eyes were closed, his face calm. From the sound of Tag's slow, shallow breathing, Walker knew that his friend had fallen asleep. He sat down next to Tag, easing his tired back against the rough wall.

Feeling Great Owl's eyes on him, Walker stared straight ahead, not wanting to meet the old Seer's gaze. The smell of cooking fires drifted in the air. Sounds of tired voices mingled with the song of a chickadee. The air was cooling down. The canyon's harsh, rocky cliffs mellowed in the late-day shadows. Walker closed his eyes. *Náat, my uncle, you have sent me here. What must I do here, among these people that seem so much like our Hopi brothers and sisters?*

The sound of excited voices started to ripple in the evening air. Walker opened his eyes and listened as they seemed to draw near. He looked over at Great Owl. The Seer's eyes still rested on him yet seemed to be hundreds of miles or years away.

"Son of Great Bear!"

"Son of Great Bear is coming."

"But he travels alone."

"Lone Eagle is not with him!" The news was being called from one home to the next, the anxious words being carried on the wind.

Small Cub rushed out his door, his smiling face filled with excitement. His mother followed more slowly. Her eyes, filled with worried anticipation, looked down the trail. Resting her hands on her huge belly, she rubbed them together.

Flute Maiden came out of her door and peered down the trail. Using his staff, Great Owl struggled to his feet and moved to her side. Walker nudged Tag and stood up to look down the trail.

"What?" asked Tag in a drowsy voice, looking around. "I was just getting comfortable." Hearing the relay of calls and seeing everyone standing and watching the trail, he tried to scramble to his feet. "I'm stiff all over," he mumbled, finally getting his long, thin body up. "What's happening?" he asked, at Walker's elbow.

Before Walker could answer, a man came into view on the trail. He was a little taller than Walker, muscular, yet thin at the same time. His long, black hair, with a white eagle feather tied in it, flowed down to his waist. He had a handsome, square face with heavy eyebrows above large, quick, black eyes. He carried a spear in one arm and a bow slung over the opposite shoulder. His face, chest, and legs were caked with dust and sweat. He took long sure strides toward them.

"Father, Father!" cried Small Cub, running down the trail toward the man.

Son of Great Bear raised a hand in greeting to the others. He swept Small Cub up into his arms, hugging him. "Well, my son, you have grown a foot since I left last moon!" his words carried in the wind.

Clinging to his father's neck, Small Cub squealed, "I have grown. I have. I can run faster than Running Boy! Well, almost."

Laughing, Son of Great Bear set his son down. Taking his small son's hand and moving up the trail, he said, "That I must see."

"And we have strangers—visitors at our house. Well, Grandfather's house. One is all speckled and talks in strange words, and he . . ."

"Hush, my son," said Son of Great Bear, a few feet from his home.

Walker felt the man scrutinizing him as he walked closer to the group of people waiting for him. After a few seconds, Son of Great Bear's eyes darted toward Tag. They grew wider and more concerned. Then his gaze fell upon Morning Flower. A smile flashed across his face. His steps became faster.

While Walker watched Son of Great Bear greet Morning Flower with a warm hug, he whispered to Tag, "It's Morning Flower's husband, Son of Great Bear. He must have been with Chief Lone Eagle, on the sacred mountain. For some reason, he has come back without him."

"Do you think the chief is dead or something?" asked Tag. Before Walker could answer, they heard someone approaching in the opposite direction. Turning, he saw White Badger and Scar Cheek coming up the trail from the hidden entrance. Both their faces held anxious concern.

"Son of Great Bear! Welcome back," said White Badger, taking long strides toward his brother-in-law. Scar Cheek stopped next to Walker, but his total attention was on the other two men.

"It is good to be back with our family," replied Son of Great Bear with a bright smile, "and to find all is well here." His face became suddenly solemn. He reached out to place his hand on White Badger's shoulder. "I have an important message for you, the Warrior Chief of our people," his voice was low and grave. Turning his head to face Great Owl, he continued, "I also have one for you, father-in-law. Both are concerning Lone Eagle." Tears sparkled in his eyes.

The mysterious feeling rushed toward Walker, engulfing him in a giant wave, whispering, "Death is near . . ."

# 15

They sat in a close circle in the center of Great Owl's home. Light from the small fire in the cooking pit flickered and swayed, casting eerie shadows against the limestone walls. A small, ceramic bowl with a lighted wick floating in some sort of dark, thick fat was placed in the middle of the circle. From its illumination, Walker could see the faces around him.

Son of Great Bear's handsome, strong face was lined with fatigue from his hurried journey home. His eyes held uncertainty as he stole quick glances at Tag, Walker, and the turquoise pendant hanging on Walker's chest.

White Badger talked in whispers to Son of Great Bear. There were signs of tension around his mouth and eyes. It was plain to see that he was anxious to hear his brother-in-law's message.

Tag looked tired, yet alert and curious. He had eaten his share of stew and small corncakes. With his hunger stilled, he seemed eager to get on with Son of Great Bear's news. Walker had been given permission to translate all that was to be said to him.

Flute Maiden's face seemed even more delicate and beautiful in the dim, flickering light. Only her lips, pressed together, showed any indication of concern. Meeting Walker's glance, she smiled. The candlelight danced and twinkled in her dark eyes.

Great Owl's face was unreadable. He sat as the others, with his legs crossed in front of him, his hands resting on his knees. His black eyes stared into the glow of the candle. Walker gazed into the small flame, trying to see what Great Owl's eyes saw. All he could see was the small, yellow gleam burning against the darkness.

Soft voices outside the doorway brought Walker's head up. Morning Flower crawled through the low entrance. "Small Cub is finally asleep. With so much happening today, he had a hard time." With Son of Great Bear's help, she sat down next to him. Walker saw love in her eyes as she looked into her husband's face. "Scar Cheek is outside the door. He will listen for Small Cub," she said.

*And, he will keep watch to make sure that no one is spying on us,* thought Walker, feeling tension starting to build within his body.

Since the moment of his return, Son of Great Bear had not been alone with family. Men and women had flocked to welcome him home. Some came seeking news of their husbands or sons who were still on the sacred mountain; all came to hear news of their chief, Lone Eagle.

Son of Great Bear had greeted each person with warmth and confidence. He gave assurances to all that the men were on their way back home, but nothing had been said about Lone Eagle.

He had met Gray Wolf's hostile assault of prying questions and vehement demands with an unshakable strength and calmness. He did not give Gray Wolf any more information than he gave the others. At last Gray Wolf, his face twisted in anger, had left.

Now after eating a quick meal and with Scar Cheek standing guard outside, Son of Great Bear was about to deliver his messages. He looked across to his father-in-law. "Great Owl, I will deliver Lone Eagle's message to you first." Son of Great Bear's voice was low but strong. "I, Lone Eagle, send greetings to Great Owl, my good friend of many years . . ."

By the intonation of Son of Great Bear's voice, Walker could tell that he had memorized the chief's verbal message word by word. Walker whispered the translation to Tag.

"My heart is with you and my people at this perilous time. My daily prayers are for you." Son of Great Bear paused as if to indicate a new paragraph or a different train of thought. "My bones grow weaker with each setting sun though my heart is strong, my mind clear." Son of Great Bear's eyes met Great Owl's.

Great Owl nodded. A look of resigned sadness filled his eyes.

Son of Great Bear continued at a pace that allowed Walker to interpret. "The holy spirits living here on Nuvatukya'ovi, our sacred mountain, have answered my many prayers. The way to save our people from hunger, sickness, and death has been made known to me. My time and our people's time is short. I feel the presence of Masau'u, that great and terrible spirit of death, drawing nearer with each sunrise. I do not tremble at meeting death myself, but for my beloved people I fear." Son of Great Bear paused; his eyes glistened with tears. His voice was soft but firm as he finished. "Great Owl, my trusted friend and Seer, now is the time. Now is the time that we have spoken of so often in whispers, hopes, and fears. Now is the time for your holiest prayers and strongest powers."

Silence filled the room. Every eye was on Great Owl. Tears stood in the old man's eyes. He looked across at Walker. Walker felt his scalp tighten. A tingling sensation worked its way up his back.

A loud popping sound from the fire broke the intense silence.

"Lone Eagle's message is clear," said Great Owl in a low voice, "and all has been done."

Son of Great Bear drew in a deep breath of air and let it out. He looked relieved, but his eyes still reflected worry. Turning to his brother-in-law, he went on, "White Badger, our chief sends you this message." Again Son of Great Bear's manner of speaking changed as he recited the words he had memorized. "To White Badger, our people's chosen Warrior Chief, I send you greetings. At tomorrow's first light, my men and I will leave the sacred mountain and start the journey home." Son of Great Bear paused.

When he continued, it was in a very low voice. "I am sending Son of Great Bear ahead to give you this warning. The days ahead will be full of strife. Be strong in your leadership over our people in my absence. Beware of him that hungers for power, like a hungry wolf stalking his prey. He would go to great extremes to seize any and all authority. Under his selfish leadership our people would die a slow, agonizing death." Son of Great Bear stopped.

White Badger's eyes were clear, his face set firmly. He nodded his head, the meaning of the warning understood.

Son of Great Bear continued the message, "The time draws near when you must stand united with the one chosen to be the new chief. You must be strong."

A heavy silence filled the dim walls. Each person seemed deep in his own thoughts and fears. Walker tried to piece together the two messages in his mind but couldn't. What was Lone Eagle trying to tell both Great Owl and White Badger that he couldn't just say outright?

Son of Great Bear broke the thick silence. Now that the messages were delivered, he spoke in his normal tone. "Our Chief is so weak that the men must help him walk and he must rest often. Even with this, if all goes well, they will be here in two or three sunsets."

"I must have medicine ready for him," stated Flute Maiden, beginning to rise.

"It is too late for that, little sister. Masau'u's deathly fingers are on Lone Eagle already," said Son of Great Bear, looking at her with compassion.

Flute Maiden nodded. She folded her hands in her lap, lowering her eyes to the ground. Tears washed her cheeks. Walker's heart ached seeing her so saddened.

"We must be ready when the mantle of leadership is changed," Son of Great Bear continued, looking toward Great Owl, then to White Badger. "From just the few moments that I spent with Gray Wolf today, I am afraid that there may be violence."

"Yes, all the years of hatred and bitterness boiling in his heart have made him very determined and dangerous," Great Owl stated. Meeting Walker's questioning eyes, he explained, "Long ago, before Lone Eagle became our leader, a man named Single Feather was our chief. He led our people, as his father before him, with wisdom and love for many,

many years. He began to grow little with old age. His back became stooped and weak. His eyes became clouded over. Since he had no son to become chief after him, he announced that on the next moon he would appoint one to be the new chief." Great Owl closed his eyes as in mental pain.

After a few seconds, Great Owl's eyes opened and rested upon Walker. "As is our custom, Single Feather greeted each new sun in prayer to ask for the well-being of our people. He sought rain and sun to insure plentiful crops. He prayed for many healthy children in our village. He was always the very first to offer such prayers each morning when the sky was gray before the morning light. The place he chose for these morning prayers was a ledge overlooking our canyon. Two days before he was to name the new chief, while he knelt in prayer he fell to his death."

Walker translated Great Owl's words to Tag.

"Sounds a bit suspicious," Tag whispered back to Walker. "What happened?"

As if Great Owl had understood the bahana's words, he continued, "In choosing a new chief the village became split into two groups. One group wanted Gray Wolf's father, Red Hawk. The others wanted Lone Eagle as their chief. After much disagreement and discontent, the men in the village cast feathers to determine who would be the new chief. When the feathers were counted, the greater number lay at Lone Eagle's feet. He would be the new chief. Red Hawk was bitter, but the choice had been made. This was years before Gray Wolf was born. From the day he was born, Gray Wolf was fed on his father's bitterness until his heart became filled with hatred." Great Owl gazed into Walker's eyes.

Looking back at Great Owl, Walker said, "If his father had won, Gray Wolf would be the next chief instead of Lone Eagle's son, so he feels cheated."

Great Owl nodded.

"Twice cheated," stated Son of Great Bear in a firm voice. "It is our way to let the people choose the Warrior Chief, who is second in command. The Warrior Chief is always chosen by casting feathers. Eleven moons ago, our Warrior Chief became mysteriously sick and died very fast."

"Too fast and too unnatural," whispered Flute Maiden.

Son of Great Bear continued, "Gray Wolf wanted to be the new Warrior Chief. He tried to gain the support of our men. Some did follow him. Those that didn't were threatened and accidents just seemed to happen to many of these men. Again the harmony of our people was destroyed. Only Lone Eagle's strength and wisdom held our village together until the day when the feathers were cast. On that day when the most feathers were placed at White Badger's feet, Gray Wolf swore by Masau'u that he would not be cheated a third time."

Only the soft sounds of the crackling fire filled the rock dwelling. Walker watched the small, flaming wick floating in the black-and-white ceramic bowl. The mysterious feeling had wrapped its icy fingers around him, squeezing his breath from him. The smell of death filled his nose. Masau'u was near. Walker's mind tried to fight off the suffocating feeling. "Death . . . Death . . . Death," the feeling thundered in Walker's ears and heart.

# 16

"Where is Lone Eagle's son? Why hasn't anyone introduced us?" Tag whispered to Walker in the dark. They were lying on sleeping mats next to the front wall of Great Owl's home. Great Owl, Flute Maiden, and White Badger were asleep on mats in the back of the room.

Walker answered, "I guess he is with his father. It would be natural for him to go with Lone Eagle." Even though the answer was logical, Walker had a gut feeling that it wasn't true.

"Well, maybe. Doesn't it seem strange that we haven't even heard the son's name?" Tag flopped over on his stomach. "Hey, maybe they don't want Lone Eagle's son to be chief. Maybe he's a jerk or something."

"Hmmm," Walker mumbled, pushing a strand of hair out of his eyes. That was a point he had not thought of. Maybe Tag was right. Was it possible that Great Owl and White Badger were actually plotting against Lone Eagle? Did they want Son of Great Bear to be the next chief? What kind of political intrigue had Tag and he stumbled into?

Had Great Owl saved them from Gray Wolf just so he could use them as a sacrifice later to further his own ambitions for political power? How was Flute Maiden involved in all this? Walker's heart began to beat faster. Sweat wet his forehead. Had he been too trusting of these people sleeping just a few feet from him? Were things not as they seemed to be? Which way was death coming from—both? His mind was so tired now that everything seemed unreal—like a bad dream.

Walker put his hands over his eyes. He remembered Singing Woman's words, "See with your heart." He tried to block out his thoughts, letting his feelings speak. A deep warmth began filling his heart. Of course he trusted Great Owl and his family. He had no choice but to trust them. Gray Wolf had made his intention toward him crystal clear from the very beginning.

Tag shifted his long body on the thin mat, trying to find a comfortable position. "They're not telling us something, something important." He turned completely over, flipping the mat out from under him as he did. "This ground feels like cement," he mumbled, trying to get the woven mat back under him. "It's a wonder that any of these people can even walk after sleeping like this night after night. Back in the future, I thought my mom was really mean for forcing me to make my nice, soft bed every morning. Boy, was I ever a crybaby back then."

"It sounds like you are homesick," observed Walker in a low voice.

"Of course I am not homesick." Tag's voice sounded indignant, then it softened. "Well, maybe a little, but just for my bed."

•   •   •

117

Whispers in the back of the room woke Walker. His head was still full of uneasy sleep. He heard Son of Great Bear's worried voice whispering in fast, short sentences. Flute Maiden's alert, low voice answered back.

Walker pushed up on one elbow. Seeing the doorway bathed in darkness, Walker knew that it was still night or very early morning. The cooking fire had died, leaving the room pitch black. He could hear Tag's heavy breathing beside him. From the back of the room he heard quick movements.

"Son of Great Bear, please carry this. I have everything else. Let's go," Flute Maiden's soft voice said.

Son of Great Bear crossed to the door and went out. Flute Maiden followed. When she came close to Walker, he whispered her name.

Flute Maiden knelt down next to him. "Morning Flower's baby is about to be born. I am going to help her. Son of Great Bear brought Small Cub here. He's asleep on my mat. When the others wake up, please tell them I am next door."

"Is there anything I can do?" asked Walker.

He felt Flute Maiden's warm hand touch his shoulder. "If we need anything, I will send Son of Great Bear. Thank you." Then she was gone.

Silence again filled the darkness. The four-foot rock-and-mud walls dividing the two homes muffled the sounds from next door. Walker lay back down on his mat. A cool breeze drifted through the door, bringing the dry scent of sage with it. Tag mumbled something in his sleep. A deep cough came from the back of the room, then the sound of someone turning over.

Silence.

Walker closed his eyes, but his mind was alert. He tried to reassess the situation. His thoughts went in circles and nothing fit together in a logical way. *What am I missing? What is so obvious that I can't see or feel it?*

A muffled scream reached through Walker's troubled thoughts, bringing him to his feet and out the nearby door. The cool night air brought goose bumps up on his bare chest and back.

In the bright moonlight, Walker saw Son of Great Bear come tumbling out of his doorway. Seeing Walker, he cried, "Light! Flute Maiden needs more light to see by." There was desperation in his voice. "Wood—get more wood. Hurry, hurry! Morning Flower is . . ." he couldn't finish. He brought his trembling hands to his face, shaking his head.

"Son of Great Bear!" Flute Maiden's voice from within the house was urgent. A long, painful cry followed.

"Light—get more light!" Son of Great Bear pleaded, looking at Walker. He turned and scrambled back into his house.

Walker took two giant steps, bent down, and crawled through Great Owl's doorway. With one more step he was next to his sleeping mat. In the darkness, his fingers searched for his backpack. He found Tag's foot instead. It was soft, gritty, and cold.

"What's wrong?" Tag's voice sounded as if he were talking in his sleep.

Walker's finger's felt his backpack. Grabbing it, he turned, and started toward the door. "Morning Flower is having her baby."

"Oh, is that all," Tag's voice floated back into sleep, as Walker went out the door.

Bending down again, he slipped through Son of Great Bear's doorway. In the dim light of a small fire in the corner of the room, he saw Morning Flower lying on the ground. Son of Great Bear was kneeling, holding her head in his lap. Morning Flower's cries of pain filled the air.

Flute Maiden knelt between Morning Flower's drawn-up knees. She was speaking in a soft but firm voice to her patient. "Pant, Morning Flower, pant as if you have been running. Don't push. Good. Keep panting." Tenseness filled her voice. "Something isn't right, but I can't see what. Light! I need more light!"

Walker fumbled at the buckle on his backpack. His fingers seemed thick and clumsy. His palms were wet with sweat, his fingers sticky as he got the buckle loose. Reaching inside, he felt the soft feather on the prayer stick. Gently, he dug under the fragile paho. He felt the rough, cotton flour bag that held the red cornmeal. *Spirit food.* Walker's blood suddenly felt like ice. He pushed the bag to one side of the backpack, feeling for his flashlight. Where was it? The seconds seemed like years. Groping, his fingers came in contact with hard, smooth steel. With quick steps, Walker moved toward Flute Maiden. Flicking the flashlight on, he knelt down beside her. "Is this enough light?"

Flute Maiden gazed at the unknown source of bright light for a split second, then returned to her work. "Yes, now I can see what must be done," her voice trailed off.

Walker held the light steady. Morning Flower cried out in agony.

"No, don't push. Don't push—not yet," ordered Flute Maiden. "Pant!"

The seconds became hours. Walker's forehead was wet,

and his heart beat against his chest as he watched Flute Maiden work. *In these primitive conditions how many women die in childbirth? How many babies survive?* "Great Tawaa," he prayed silently, "guide Flute Maiden's hands and mind."

"Good," Flute Maiden's voice sounded confident. "Now things are as they should be."

Within minutes, a healthy cry filled the home. A tiny, beautiful daughter with black, downy hair lay in Morning Flower's loving arms.

Walker slipped outside unnoticed. The sky was growing gray with early morning light. The moon and its sister star hung in the far west. Walker closed his eyes and breathed deeply. The air smelled clean, fresh—new.

"My son," Great Owl's voice sounded like a gentle breeze in the pines.

Walker turned to see the old man standing outside his house. "You have a new granddaughter," Walker said, warmth filling his heart.

"Then we have much to thank Taawa for this morning." Great Owl moved slowly down the trail. Walker followed.

He led Walker to a flat, rocky ledge overlooking the canyon. Using his carved staff, Great Owl knelt. Then he lifted his arms toward the sky and closed his eyes. In a deep, throaty voice, he began to sing a prayer of thanks.

Here prayers are also offered to the first rays of sun each day, just as it is done at my village, Walker thought. He knelt down not far from Great Owl. His mind and heart were full. For the first time since Náat's death, Walker felt joy in living. He had seen a new life begin and he had helped in his own small way. Was this the reason he had been sent back here—to help this small infant into the world? Would she play a significant role in her people's future? If this was the reason he had been sent, it was enough. With a smile, Walker closed his eyes to pray.

Finishing his prayer, Walker opened his eyes. He spit over his right shoulder. Now he was cleansed and ready to start a new day. He rose to his feet. Great Owl was still kneeling. Walker stood listening to his deep, humble voice petitioning for guidance.

Suddenly Walker felt the hair on his neck rise. With a swift movement he jerked around toward the trail. Standing there with a smirk on his face and hatred burning his eyes stood Gray Wolf. He held a spear in one hand, while his other hand rested on the knife strapped on his waist. "I will not be cheated a third time," he growled just loud enough for Walker to hear. Giving a short snort, he turned and stalked out of sight.

". . . while saying his morning prayers, he fell to his death . . ." The words spoken the night before echoed in Walker's mind.

# 17

The news of the baby's birth spread like the sun's early morning rays. Even before Great Owl's household had finished eating a meager breakfast of small, round corncakes, village women began to arrive next door at Son of Great Bear's house.

Standing just inside Great Owl's door, Walker watched small groups of women, two or three at a time, come walking up the trail. Each woman carried a large, ceramic bowl or pot slung over one hip. Upon reaching Son of Great Bear's door, the women patiently waited outside until Son of Great Bear came out to greet them and to invite them in. Sometimes a group had to wait five or ten minutes until the women in the previous group left. While waiting, the women visited and laughed in soft voices. Walker recognized most of them by name.

"What's happening?" Tag asked, looking over Walker's shoulder. He shoved the last bit of a corncake into his mouth. His hair was a tangled mane of curls. But somehow his freckled face was clean.

"Women are coming to see Morning Flower's baby." Walker moved a bit so Tag could see out the doorway.

Tag watched. "I guess a new baby always attracts women. What are they all carrying in the big pots?"

Walker shrugged his shoulders.

Three women holding empty pots emerged from Son of Great Bear's door. They spoke to the two women waiting outside, then left. Before the other two women could enter Son of Great Bear's doorway, Small Cub came tumbling out. He came barreling into Great Owl's home, almost knocking over Walker and Tag. Looking up, his face broke into a huge grin. "Father says that I must bring you to see my new sister!"

"We would be honored to come," Walker answered, ruffling the little boy's thick, black hair.

"Small Cub, please tell your mother that I will be over in a few minutes," Flute Maiden called from the back of the room where she was tidying things up. "Is Great Owl at your house now?" she asked.

Small Cub nodded. "Grandfather and Uncle White Badger both came, but Uncle left." Taking Tag's hand, Small Cub began pulling him out the doorway.

Son of Great Bear greeted them at his door. "Welcome to my house. Please come in and share in this special day."

Morning Flower lay close to the back of the room, covered with a blanket made from strips of animal skins woven together. Great Owl sat cross-legged on a mat close to Morning Flower. Small Cub pulled Tag toward them. "Hurry before she starts crying again. She loves to cry."

"Brother," Son of Great Bear said to Walker. "I did not get to thank you before you left earlier. Without your help, Morning Flower and my daughter might have . . ." his voice faltered.

"I was proud to help," Walker said in a low voice. His eyes met Son of Great Bear's and saw acceptance reflected in the intelligent, dark eyes.

Walker knelt beside Tag and Small Cub by Morning Flower's mat. Morning Flower smiled shyly. She pulled back the edge of the white rabbitskin that covered the small bundle in her arms.

Walker's heart filled with wonder as he looked at the small, dark, wrinkled face framed by the soft fur. The baby's eyes were closed. Her small, heart-shaped mouth moved as if it were sucking. A tiny, perfect fist lay against her round, smooth cheek.

"She doesn't like to have her eyes open," stated Small Cub, still holding Tag's hand. He crunched up his face into a scowl. "I think she's funny looking," he whispered to Tag. As if he had understood, Tag smiled and nodded. Walker tried hard not to laugh.

"What are you going to name her?" Tag asked, squeezing Small Cub.

Walker conveyed the question. Shaking his head, Small Cub squealed with laughter. "Big brothers don't name babies—aunts do!"

It was also a Hopi tradition to have a maternal aunt choose an infant's first name. How similar the two cultures are, thought Walker, turning to Tag. "You will have to ask Flute Maiden if she has chosen a name yet for the baby."

Tag rubbed his chin. "Hmmm, just like the Hopis do, right?" he asked, as if he were entering it into his mental journal of living archaeology.

Walker just nodded, surprised again at Tag's knowledge of his people's ways.

Watching the baby and listening to Small Cub's chatter, Walker became aware of movement in back of him. Looking over his shoulder, he saw two women working in the front corner of the room by the doorway. After a few seconds of watching them, he nudged Tag's arm. Tag turned. Walker nodded toward the women.

Littlest Star was bending down, reaching into the big pot at her feet. Her hands came out cradling dark, wet mud. With quick, smooth movements, she spread the mud out over the wall. The other woman, Fawn, was also plastering the wall with mud from her large bowl.

"It is a tradition to make our homes as fresh as possible after the birth of child," Morning Flower said in a soft voice. Walker realized that it was the first time she had spoken directly to him. "It is our way of showing respect and gratitude for the new life among us." Morning Flower's tired face looked pleased as she watched her friends work. "By nightfall, all the walls will have a new layer of plaster."

"Everywhere except there," said Small Cub, jumping up and running over to the door. He stood pointing to a spot over the doorway where Walker could vaguely see something with a small feather tied to it.

Son of Great Bear explained, "When our daughter's birth cord dries up and falls off, I will tie it to a small prayer stick. Then I will wedge the prayer stick in the wall above the doorway just below the smoke holes."

Still pointing to the spot above the doorway, Small Cub exclaimed, "Father put mine right there, so that I will always know where my true home is." With a proud smile, Small Cub ran back and plopped down into his father's lap.

"At my village, we do the same thing," Walker said, "except we put the prayer stick into the woven reeds in our open beam ceilings. We, too, always know where our hearts began and where they belong."

"Our people's ways are very much alike," Great Owl said, his deep eyes resting on Walker.

The mysterious feeling began to swirl around Walker like smoke from a fire. "Very much alike . . . alike . . . alike . . ." it whispered.

"Come on, Walker. I think we'd better leave so Morning Flower can feed her baby or whatever," Tag said, poking Walker in the ribs. He stood up and moved to the door.

Walker rose. The mysterious feeling faded away. "Thank you for sharing your daughter with us," he said to Morning Flower. "She is beautiful." Morning Flower smiled and lowered her eyes.

Son of Great Bear touched his arm. "I think it would be best if this were hidden," he whispered, handing Walker the flashlight. "Our people are not accustomed to seeing the sunlight captured."

Taking his flashlight, Walker answered, "You are right. I'm sure that Gray Wolf could explain it in one word: witchcraft. Thank you for trusting me."

White Badger and Scar Cheek stood waiting outside on the trail. White Badger turned to Son of Great Bear. "Most of the men have left for the fields. We will also go up on the rim today to help them. There is still much being said about our visitors," White Badger said in a low voice. He looked worried as he spoke to Walker. "I think it is best that you stay close to Scar Cheek and me for the day. Where is Tag now?"

127

Walker looked around. "He must be in Son of Great Bear's house still. I thought he went out before I did. I'll go . . ."

Tag came crawling out of Son of Great Bear's low doorway. Seeing the others waiting for him, he grinned sheepishly. "What's up?" he asked, wiping his very muddy hands on his loincloth.

Walker looked at Tag's muddy hands. What had Tag been doing? Would he ever understand this bahana? He shrugged his shoulders a bit and quickly explained to Tag what White Badger had proposed.

Tag's sheepish face broke into his toothy grin. "Great! Now maybe we can meet the chief's son."

Turning to his brother-in-law, White Badger instructed, "You must stay here with your family, Son of Great Bear. I will stop at Arrow Maker's home to let him know that you are here. Send word through him if there is any trouble."

．　．　．

Arrow Maker greeted them at his door. "Welcome. Welcome," he said.

Walker recognized Arrow Maker as the man with the yellow cape and the limp who had told Scar Cheek about the men meeting at the fort yesterday. Without his long cape on, Walker could now see that Arrow Maker's right leg was thinner and shorter than his left leg. His left shoulder hunched forward from a large hump on his back. "Sit. Sit," he said, easing himself down with some difficulty onto a mat just outside his doorway.

White Badger knelt down beside the middle-aged man. The others did the same, making a small circle.

"You need arrows," said Arrow Maker, and a proud smile filled his small, round face. A neat row of smooth, straight arrow shafts lay near him on one side. On the other side was a tidy line of completed arrows with sharp, black obsidian arrowheads. Spread out in front of him was a leather cloth with the tools of his trade lying on it. Arrow Maker picked up one of the unfinished shafts and began working on it with a small, stone knife.

Walker heard Tag catch his breath. He knew without even looking that Tag's eyes were bulging at what he was seeing.

"Yes, my friend, we need arrows. Tomorrow we will leave before sunrise to hunt. Since we must have only the truest of arrows, we come to you, of course," said White Badger, with a smile in his voice. Leaning close to Arrow Maker, he reached down and picked up a completed arrow. While inspecting it, he continued in a low voice. "We will be in the fields today. Our visitors will be with us, but Son of Great Bear will remain behind with his family. *Others* will remain behind, too, I am sure."

The tone of White Badger's voice made Arrow Maker look up from his work. It was clear that he had understood White Badger. He nodded. His eyes glanced toward Tag. Tag flashed him a friendly grin, which Arrow Maker returned. He turned to Walker, still smiling. He noticed the eagle pendant around Walker's neck. Arrow Maker's eyes widened, his thin lips becoming a firm, straight line across his face. He studied the turquoise pendant. His mouth opened slightly as if he were about to say something to Walker.

Instead, Arrow Maker turned to White Badger and Scar Cheek. "My son will stay here and work with me today. He is helping his mother get water now, but he will be back soon. His legs are fast and strong for one only eight summers. He will find you if you are needed here," Arrow Maker's voice was a whisper.

"Good," said White Badger in a normal tone. "These are excellent arrows, as always."

Arrow Maker laughed. "As always—of course." He reached down and picked up the finished arrows. Their sharp, black points caught the morning light. "Will this be enough?"

Taking the arrows, White Badger answered, "For now, yes, but there may be a need for more soon."

Arrow Maker nodded his head in understanding, and a worried look washed over his face. Walker's scalp tightened as a chill worked its way up his back.

"Walker, ask him if I can come back sometime to watch him make arrows," Tag whispered, his voice full of excitement.

"My friend admires your work," Walker said, nodding toward the unfinished arrows. "He would like to come back and watch you work."

A grin spread across Arrow Maker's face. "My legs and back are crooked and weak, but these hands," he said, lifting his hands up, "can make arrows that shoot straight and true."

"You also make the keenest spearheads and the best knives in the village," added Scar Cheek.

Arrow Maker chuckled with pleasure. "Tell your friend that I would be honored if he came back anytime. I will teach him all he wants to know."

Walker translated his offer to Tag. "Great! Tell him I will be back as soon as I can. Learning to make arrows—I can't believe it!" Tag exclaimed. "This is getting better and better."

Watching the bahana's excitement, Arrow Maker grinned and nodded his head. Tag had won another friend, thought Walker.

As they rose to leave, Arrow Maker reached out and touched Walker's arm. "Wait," he said in a firm voice. Walker paused. Arrow Maker reached into a leather pouch sitting next to his tools. He drew out a six-inch black stone. Handing it to Walker, he said, "You will need a good knife."

Walker looked down at the crude weapon in his hand. The black obsidian had been flaked at one end to fit into a hand snugly. The other end had been shaped and sharpened to a fine point. He ran his finger along the sharp edge of the knife to its point. It was simplistic, undeveloped, but it would be very effective in skinning a rabbit or deer. It would also offer a degree of protection. Walker turned it over in his hand. It fit perfectly. He was stunned by Arrow Maker's generosity.

Before Walker could speak, Arrow Maker handed a second knife to Tag. It was smaller, but still a formidable tool and weapon. Tag was speechless as he examined his gift. "I can't believe it, just can't believe it," he finally said in almost a whisper. "Thank you—thank you." His grin covered his freckled face.

Walker slipped his knife under the thick, leather thong around his waist. The keen blade lay against the brown buckskin loincloth that White Badger had lent him to wear. Its black polished surface almost glistened in the sun. "We owe you much for these beautiful knives," Walker said to Arrow Maker. "Thank you."

"You will earn them, I think," Arrow Maker said with a strange sound of confidence in his voice.

The image of Gray Wolf's lean face flashed through Walker's mind, followed by the vision of the black knife bathed in bright red blood.

# 18

Walker was glad that he was wearing the short, leather loincloth instead of the long leggings that Náat had sent with him. Even though it was still early morning, the sun's rays were very hot.

Walker felt anxious following White Badger up the steep, narrow path leading to the rim of the canyon. It would be good to be out of the limestone walls and to be able to see the sacred mountain once more. What would it look like now, seven hundred years ago? he wondered.

With no physical warning, they crested the canyon's rim. White Badger stopped to talk to the man standing guard at the trail head. As they talked, the man's deeply slant eyes kept glancing at Walker and Tag, his fingers gripping his spear. Walker could see suspicion and fear in the man's face.

"Gosh," gasped Tag, looking around. "I can't believe the difference!" Taking a few steps, with his arms making a sweeping motion, he continued. "This used to be—I mean this will be—forest for as far as you can see. But now it's just, just . . ."

"Rocky, dry farmland," finished Walker, brushing a strand of hair out of his sweaty face.

The area nearby had been cleared of rocks and neatly terraced. Groups of men and boys were working among the crops planted in the different terraces. Around the terraces, the earth became studded with mounds of limestone rocks. Cacti and sage were the only vegetation growing among the rocks.

Walker shaded his eyes from the sun looking toward the San Francisco Peaks. His breath caught in his throat. The silhouette of the sacred mountain, made up of its three, partially coned-shaped, volcanic peaks, was the same as he had always known it. But the mountain's face and sides were alien to him. Instead of being covered with the green softness of thick forest, its sides were hardened black with deep, massive lava flows. The holy mountain stood out harsh and hostile looking against the brilliant blue sky. A thin layer of clouds shrouded the mountain's top. Small batches of puffy clouds floated away from the blanket of clouds lying on the highest peaks.

"I just can't believe it," Tag repeated. "Everything is so different. The only things that look the least bit familiar are the clouds on the San Francisco Peaks."

"Not clouds; Kachinas," whispered Walker so quietly that his friend couldn't hear his words. He wouldn't take time now to explain to this twentieth-century bahana that the clouds leaving the sacred mountain were actually the friendly spirits that the Hopi called Kachinas or Cloud People. These guardian spirits of the Hopis lived on the holy mountain's highest peak. But during the months of spring and summer, they became clouds floating to the Hopi mesas to hear the prayers of the people. These humble pleas asked for plentiful sun and rain to insure good crops; for strength and good health for all who lived in the villages; and most important, for peace and harmony.

Walker remembered Tag saying that he had attended a day-long Kachina dance at the Hopi village. Of course Tag had watched the long rows of colorful Kachinas in the plaza as they danced to the sounds of drums, rattles, and ancient prayer songs. How much had his father told him about the sacred powers of the Kachinas? Did Tag know that at dusk when the dances were completed the Kachinas carried the prayers of the day to the gods? Then the rains would come. The crops would grow, and the Hopi people would survive another winter. It had been the ritual of Hopi life for hundreds and hundreds of years. Without the Kachina dances, the Hopis would never survive in their harsh desert environment.

A thought flashed through Walker's mind with the strength of lightning. Did the ancient ones have Kachina dances? Did they even know of these guardian spirits living so near? Walker watched another wisp of cloud break away from the sacred mountain. With the beauty and eloquence only a Kachina could have, it drifted northeast toward the Hopi mesas. Walker looked at the fields before him. He shook his head. No, the ancient ones knew nothing of the Cloud People. There were no dances here; no proper prayers to be carried to the gods by the Kachinas, so the gods did not send rain.

Of course! Náat had sent him here to give these people the secret knowledge and power of the Kachinas! Walker suddenly felt a sense of relief in possibly knowing why he had been sent.

Without a doubt Walker knew that these people needed to be under the protective care of the Kachinas or they would not survive. How could he teach such powerful and strange beliefs among these ancient brothers? The sense of relief began to fade and was replaced by fear. Gray Wolf would brand any new ideas or ways as witchcraft! Could the others possibly accept the foreign ideas and actions? How long could he survive advocating such startling concepts and practices?

"Come on, Walker," said Tag, poking his ribs. "I think it's time to earn our keep."

Walker fell in behind Tag, who followed White Badger and Scar Cheek into the terraced fields. In the first level, small, squatty corn plants were growing. Their leaves were brownish and thirsty looking. Instead of being planted in long rows, individual plants were staggered four to five feet apart. Each plant had at least a fifteen-inch-wide catch bowl dug around the base of it.

"Wouldn't it be easier if they just planted all the plants close together in nice straight rows?" Tag asked, walking between the sorry-looking plants.

"Sure, if there were plenty of water for irrigation," answered Walker. "When there isn't, it is better if each plant can spread its roots out in all directions to get any moisture there is."

"Makes sense," Tag observed. "Making such big catch bowls helps, too, I bet. In a good rainstorm the entire bowl would fill up."

Just ahead, two boys about ten years old were on their knees pulling weeds. As White Badger approached them, they continued to work, but their curious eyes darted quick glances at the approaching strangers.

"Your work is good," White Badger said, kneeling down

next to one of the boys. "No weed will steal water from your corn." The boy smiled. White Badger stood up. The boy rose with him. The other boy moved closer to White Badger. "These are our visitors, Walker and Tag."

Tag grinned and reached out to shake. Walker groaned inside. The boys stared at the large, freckled, outstretched hand. One stepped back a few inches. The other one looked as if he might bolt away any second. Tag's grin faded. He lowered his hand, letting it hang limply at his side. The awkward situation ended when White Badger called each boy by name, asking about their families and their needs. They answered his questions in turn. White Badger listened, as he did to the men of the village, with honest interest and concern. The boys' fear seemed to melt away.

In the next terrace, corn and beans were planted in a zigzagged fashion. Looking at the scraggly plants, Walker knew that this year's harvest would be very small. Even if heavy rains came soon, it would not help much, as it was too late in the growing season.

Four men were working in the next terrace among small squash plants. Each worked with a stone hoe to clear and deepen the water catches around each plant. When the group walked into the terrace, three of the men put down their tools and moved toward them. The fourth man, whom Walker recognized as one of Gray Wolf's men, continued working, but he kept his eyes on the group.

White Badger spoke to each man by name, introducing them to the boys. Tag nodded and smiled, his hands hanging at his sides. Walker met each man's eyes with friendly frankness. The men began to discuss what needed to be done in this field. Walker became aware that the fourth man had moved within a few feet of them. He was listening to what was being said as he hoed the catch bowl of a wilted squash plant. He was a small man with a very broad nose.

"Fast Lizard," White Badger said, turning to the man, "do you think that the water catches need to be redug in the far east fields?"

Fast Lizard's hardened eyes softened. Taking long steps toward the group, he answered, "Yes. But the corn just north of it needs to be weeded first."

"You are right. It will be started today. How is your son? Has he taken his first steps yet?" White Badger asked with a smile.

Fast Lizard's eyes brightened. "Yes, I am afraid that my wife will have little rest now." Everyone chuckled. All tension in the air was blown away.

By the time the sun stood high in the sky, they had visited seven other large, terraced fields along the rim of the canyon. Each one was the same: well cared for, yet dying from the lack of water. Walker and Tag were introduced to each man and boy working in the fields. Walker could see that White Badger had the same talent of winning people's confidence that his sister, Flute Maiden, had shown. He was a man whom these ancient farmers respected and trusted as their Warrior Chief and friend.

When the sun stood directly overhead, all the men gathered together to eat under a large sun shade at the very edge of the canyon. The sun shade's frame consisted of four tall poles standing in the ground. For its roof, more long poles were strapped together, and dried branches were placed over them to provide shade. Its four sides were open, and breeze came out of the canyon, fanning the hot men.

"Boy, am I starved," exclaimed Tag, "and thirsty." He

plopped down next to Walker and Scar Cheek. "Great picnic spot," he said looking up at the sun shade. "Hope the potato salad is fresh."

While cracking and eating handfuls of pinyon nuts, the twenty-five or so men and boys visited with each other. Walker sat listening and watching each face. With hunger in their stomachs and worry in their voices, they discussed the lack of rain and the poor hunting. Gradually the conversation turned to their aging chief, Lone Eagle, and his expected return. White Badger skillfully swayed the discussion to the good hunting of the years past.

With subtle humor, the men began swapping unbelievable tales of huge bears, enormous deer, giant turkeys, and monstrous rabbits. In a low voice, Walker interpreted each story to Tag. Tag's eyes grew large with wonder and amusement as he listened spellbound. Walker could tell that the men were enjoying seeing the bahana's reactions, and each saga became more unbelievable than the last. The men's suspicions and fear of the two strangers began to crumble under the sounds of laughter.

After eating, all the men worked together in one especially large field that had been terraced into six sections. Dividing into small groups, they worked together weeding and repairing the catch bowls.

Wiping the sweat from his eyes, Walker sat back on his knees to watch his friend, some ten feet away. Tag was working with the first two young boys they had met that morning. They were all kneeling around a plant. Tag and one of the boys were weeding while the third worked on the catch bowl. The three seemed to be communicating through a strange mixture of words, grunts, and some sort of sign language. Every few minutes, their laughter filled the air.

*Tag must be telling them some of his hunting stories,* thought Walker, turning his attention to a stubborn weed clinging to the ground. Pulling at the base of the weed with a twist, Walker whispered, "This one's roots must go down at least a foot. Why are there always weeds, even when there isn't enough water for the corn to grow?" The weed came out in his hand with a quick jerk. Walker almost fell backward. Catching himself, he snorted. This was the worst part of farming. He had always hated weeding. He chuckled. *I'm fighting a seven-hundred year-old war against weeds!* he thought, throwing the weed as far as he could. Wiping the sweat from his forehead, he scanned the scene before him.

Scar Cheek, along with ten other men, was in an area at the far side of the field. White Badger and the remaining workers were busy just a few yards away. The noise of stone hoes scratching at hardened, parched soil mingled with the sound of busy voices. The harsh cawing of a raven broke through the hot air. Voices died as everyone listened to the mocking laugh of the great bird. Abruptly silence filled the fields. A second later the large, black bird glided overhead, casting its eerie shadow on the dying crops.

A new, more assuring song filled the air. Starting out low where White Badger worked, it grew as each man and boy joined in the deep, throaty song. Walker recognized the rhythm of the song. The words were a bit different from the ones the Hopi farmers sang in their corn fields. Yet these words spoke the same plea for plentiful rain to raise the heads of each plant. Walker hummed the tune as he worked on another weed. He was filled with the same strong brotherly bond that he had felt at home among the Hopi men working in their fields.

Out of the corner of his eye, movement caught his attention. The skin on his back crawled. Looking up, Walker saw Gray Wolf and three armed men standing at the edge of the field. He felt their eyes on him. The smell of rotting flesh played in the hot breeze.

.    .    .

Tag groaned, easing himself down on his sleeping mat. Even in the dim light of Great Owl's home, Walker could see Tag's face wince in pain. "A bit stiff and sore," he stated, watching his friend, from his own mat.

"Why would I be? I only weeded the ancient ones' entire corn crop today," quipped Tag, rubbing the back of his aching calves. His stomach growled. "Quiet," he said, pressing on his belly. He stretched himself out on the yucca mat, closing his eyes.

Only a few inches from him, Walker studied his face. A single tear rolled out from under the bahana's long eyelashes and started to slide down the freckled cheek. Walker's heart tightened. "I miss my home, too," he said in a warm voice.

With his eyes still closed, Tag quickly wiped away the tear. He sniffed and took a deep breath. He opened his eyes. Looking into Walker's sympathetic face, he said, "I guess I am a little homesick. Sometimes I think that I will probably never see my mom and dad again." His stomach rumbled. "Or eat pizza!"

Walker nodded his head in understanding but remained quiet. His warm eyes encouraged Tag to go on.

"I really do like it here. The ancient ones are so, so— oh, I don't know. They are so much like the people seven hundred years from now. They laugh, cry, love, and worry about their kids just like my parents do—or did." Tag blinked to clear away the tears glistening in his eyes.

Walker nodded. He knew what Tag was saying was true.

"I guess all people are basically the same no matter when or where you are." Tag chuckled. "You know I always wanted a kid brother just like Small Cub." Tag pushed up on one elbow. "If I ever do get back home, I am going to talk to my parents about that," he sounded very determined.

Walker laughed. "Great Owl reminds me a lot of my uncle. If I close my eyes while he is talking, I can't really tell if it is Great Owl or Náat speaking." He felt tears stinging his eyes.

Silence.

"What's going to happen to these people, Walker? Their crops are dying. There's hardly any water to drink."

"There isn't enough wood around to burn this winter for warmth," added Walker. His chest felt heavy, as if a fifty-pound bag of worry had been placed on it.

"And as my mom would say, the sanitation facilities are far from the best. Maybe that's why there is so much sickness among them. How much longer can they survive here?" Tag asked, lying back down again with another groan.

Walker shrugged his shoulders. Gray Wolf's face, twisted with hatred, burst into his mind. "How much longer can we survive here?" he said flatly.

Silence.

"Well, maybe the new chief will like us and want to keep us around a while. Hey!" Tag shot back up. "We didn't meet Lone Eagle's son. So he must be with his father."

"I don't think so," Walker answered. Suddenly he felt very weary. "I got the distinct impression from the men today that he's not with Lone Eagle. In fact, no one seems to know where he is."

# 19

The canyon's rim was bathed in a grayish predawn light. With long, silent strides White Badger and Walker worked their way eastward along the rim. White Badger followed a path among the rocks, cacti, and sage brush. Long bows were slung over their shoulders. Quivers of arrows hung next to the stone knives at their waists. Carved, wooden rabbit-hunting sticks lay ready in their right hands.

Growling, Walker's stomach began to wake up. They had left the security of Great Owl's home without food, stopping only to offer prayers with their fast. They had started up out of the darkened canyon with only the moonlight illuminating their way.

Waves of long, thin, pewter-colored clouds outlined the eastern horizon. As the sun's rays struck the clouds, they turned pink, then burst into a brilliant red within a matter of seconds. Walker stopped, watching the beautiful transformation. His heart was filled with the beauty and peace that he felt around him.

"It's a good sign," White Badger stated in a whisper. "Our prayers will be answered this day."

By the time the sun lay just above the horizon, White Badger had led Walker to where the canyon walls converged. Looking down into the canyon, Walker saw the sun's rays crawling down the sheer cliffs, casting eerie, finger-like shadows. It was as if some great power was taking the canyon into its grip. A shiver crept up Walker's back. *Is this a sign, too?*

In awhile they were hiking along the rim on the opposite side of the canyon. White Badger started traveling westward, away from the barren and rocky rim. A thin, brown rabbit with enormous ears darted out from behind a rock. Its long legs leaped over the brush and cacti in its path. Before Walker could react, he heard a whirring sound. White Badger's rabbit stick hurled toward the rabbit, striking it in the head. In midleap the rabbit slumped to the ground, its neck broken.

As Walker approached the dead creature, his heart pounded with both pity for the rabbit and gladness that there would be meat to eat.

"Another good sign," said White Badger, stooping down to pick up the rabbit. "The gods have heard our prayers." With a smile, he put his hand over his growling stomach. "And our bellies."

An hour later there were four more rabbits in the woven bag tied to White Badger's wide, leather waistband. Walker was impressed at White Badger's skill with the rabbit-hunting stick. The stick was about two feet long and about four inches thick. One end of it had been carved into a handle that fit snugly into White Badger's hand. It was painted brown, with a panel of white on each end.

Inside the white panels were symbols of rabbits painted in black.

Walker was accustomed to such weapons. As had most young Hopi boys, he, too, had hunted with a rabbit stick. He could still vividly remember the day he had turned five years old and Náat had presented him with his first hunting stick.

"Now you must learn to hunt," Náat had said, putting the weapon in Walker's eager hand. That first rabbit stick had been small and had fit perfectly in his chubby hand. It, too, had been brown and white. Pointing to the black rabbit designs painted on the ends of the stick, Náat explained, "The rabbit spirits drawn here will call to our brothers the rabbit. If you hunt with a pure heart and happy thoughts, brother rabbit will hear these spirits calling him. Then it will come out of its burrow to see who is summoning it and our cooking pot will never be empty."

Hour after hour under Náat's firm supervision, Walker practiced with his rabbit stick. The stick was heavy and hard to throw, but soon Walker's arm grew strong enough to hurl it a good distance. Náat had insisted that he continue to practice long after all the other small boys grew tired and went to play other games. Walker's quickness and aim became much better than those of others his age. By the time he was seven years old, their cooking pot was never empty. However, it had been a good while since Walker had used his adult-size rabbit stick.

Now Walker saw a quick, hopping movement out of the corner of his eye. Just as fast, Walker brought his body around. With a powerful flick of his wrist, he caught the creature in midair with the stick he had borrowed from Son of Great Bear, bringing it down.

Examining the dead game, White Badger exclaimed, "This one is so fat, it will help fill two pots. You are in tune with Son of Great Bear's stick now."

Walker nodded with a smile. "Each weapon has its own spirit—its own way," he said, repeating the words he had heard his uncle say many times.

"I have not seen this many rabbits for many moons. Our prayers are indeed being answered this day," White Badger said, putting the kill in his bag. "If we see bigger game, let us hope that we are both in tune with our bows. My people have not tasted venison for many moons."

"Fresh venison would be great," Walker agreed, touching the beautifully carved bow hanging on his shoulder. Last evening, when Great Owl had placed it in his hands, his heart had jumped into his throat. The bow was identical to the one that Náat had so painstakingly carved for him when he was ten years old. The carefully painted animal designs matched those on his bow at home, and lifting the bow, Walker had discovered that even its weight and balance felt the same in his hand. The haunting feeling had washed over his body in a great wave.

Warm memories of the many hours spent with Náat learning to use his bow had filled Walker's swimming head. He had felt Náat's strong, loving arms around his shoulders as he taught Walker to aim properly. He had heard Náat's words of so long ago: "With the rabbit stick you will fill the cooking pot. With such a bow, you shall . . ." These vivid memories had been shattered and dissolved by Tag's worried voice calling him back to the present.

Now in the hot midmorning sun, as he walked beside White Badger, the words again echoed in Walker's mind. "With such a bow you shall . . ." What was the last part?

He tried to remember all the words that Náat had said that day many years ago. Another rabbit leaped out three feet in front of them. Two hunting sticks whirled through the air. Walker's stick hit the rabbit. White Badger's stick flew a mere inch over the falling animal's head.

"I think we should turn back now," White Badger said, putting the last rabbit in the bag. "I don't think it is wise to be away from the village very long." Patting the bag, his eyes twinkled. "These will flavor many stew pots tonight."

Walker chuckled. "I am sure Tag will appreciate having rabbit stew."

As they retraced their steps, the two talked. Walker felt at ease with White Badger. Their words flowed like smooth water and refreshed his weary mind. He found himself telling White Badger about his people so far away. He described his village, leaving out the twentieth-century inventions and luxuries that White Badger would not comprehend. White Badger listened intently, accepting everything that was said. The minutes passed quickly. Walker felt the bond between them grow stronger with each step. Was White Badger the one he should teach first about the Kachinas living so near on the sacred mountain? Walker found himself wondering. He felt sure that White Badger would listen with an open heart and mind.

"My throat is as dry as the ground we walk on," said White Badger as he stopped and wiped the sweat from his face.

"Mine, too," agreed Walker. He untied the leather thong across his chest that held a ceramic canteen about the size and shape of a large cucumber. The thong threaded through circular handles near each rounded end of the canteen. It was white with bold, black wave designs in a style that Walker had seen often on Hopi pottery. The canteen was capable of carrying almost half a quart of water. Walker handed it to White Badger. "You made the first kill."

With the canteen resting in one hand, White Badger pulled the carved wooden stopper out of the narrow opening at the top of the canteen with his other hand. Holding a rounded end in each hand, White Badger brought the canteen to his lips. "You made the last." He closed his eyes and drank deeply.

As he waited for his turn, Walker scanned the horizon. The sun beat down directly overhead, leaving no shadows. Everything looked flat, harsh, unreal, like a painted backdrop on a stage. His eyes skipped right past the large, still, brown shape twelve feet to the east. Then something in his mind clicked. His eyes backtracked. His heart began pounding in his ears.

Without a sound, he eased the bow off his shoulder with one hand, while the other drew out an arrow. With the arrow in place, Walker drew back the sinew string with all his strength.

"With such a bow, you will . . ." Náat's words filled his mind.

Walker aimed the crude but sharp arrowhead on the end of the straight, gamble oak wood shaft.

"With such a bow, you will . . ."

The huge buck stared in Walker's direction. Its proud head was held high, and its magnificent six-point rack pointed to the sky. Its large, dark eyes rested on Walker.

The air was filled with the whistling sound of the arrow. As Walker watched its flight, the arrow seemed to move through the air in slow motion. The seconds became centuries—one hundred years . . . three hundred years . . . five hundred years . . . seven hundred years . . .

The arrow's deadly projectile penetrated the huge buck's heart.

"With such a bow you will win the hearts of your people . . ." Náat's voice rang in Walker's ears.

# 20

Walker shifted the end of the thick pole they had cut from a dying pinyon pine from his right shoulder to his left. The buck's feet were lashed to the pole, its head and back hanging almost to the ground. White Badger and Walker each carried one end of the pole, with White Badger leading the way. They had hauled the kill less than a quarter of a mile, but Walker's back and shoulders ached. His body glistened with sweat. His mouth was parched. The weight of the buck seemed to increase with each short step.

As they neared the first of the cornfields, Walker felt sure that some of the men working there would offer to help carry the heavy buck down into the canyon. *An offer too good to refuse,* he thought, reaching up to wipe the sweat off his forehead.

"Something is wrong," White Badger said, stopping at the edge of the first field. It was empty except for the wind gently rustling among the long, wilted corn leaves. Walker could see that the next field was also abandoned. White

149

Badger set off again, taking the shortest possible route across the dying field.

Walker could feel White Badger's tension and could smell sweat, deer hide, and death in the air. There were no workers in any of the fields they passed. Walker began to feel his own anxiety build. White Badger walked even faster. Walker followed, trying not to stumble under the heavy load.

The man standing guard at the trail head had his back toward them. He was leaning on his spear, his shoulders sagging, his head slumped forward.

"Fast Lizard," White Badger called, waving.

The man whirled around. He raised his hand in welcome. Within seconds, he stood next to White Badger. "The gods must have been with you today," he said, helping them lower the buck to the ground. Kneeling down beside the magnificent creature, he inspected it. In disbelief he shook his head. "Whose arrow made the kill?"

"Walker's," White Badger stated. "The men aren't working the field." His eyes questioned.

Fast Lizard looked up, his faced lined with worry and crisscrossed with grief. "Much has happened in the few hours that you have been gone." Standing up he reported, "With the first rays of sun, Masau'u crept into our village, stalking every family with a swift and painful death." He clenched his spear. His knuckles turned white. His dark eyes spoke of personal lost. "He has claimed three spirits already: Gray Dove's mother, the youngest daughter of Scar Cheek and Littlest Star, and . . ." Fast Lizard's voice faltered, "my nephew, Running Boy."

"Your loss is great," White Badger said, touching Fast Lizard's shoulder. Walker could tell by White Badger's tight face that each life lost was a personal blow to him also.

"Many of our oldest and our youngest lie in Masau'u's fingertips," finished Fast Lizard. Fear etched deep lines in his anxious face. "My son—I am worried that he will . . ." He couldn't finish.

White Badger nodded in understanding. "We will leave the meat here. I will send some men up for it as soon as I can. I will have them bring word of your son to you." In White Badger's eyes, Walker saw the overpowering worry that he felt burning in his own heart.

Walker trotted close behind White Badger down the steep, rocky trail. His heart hammered against his chest. The now familiar names of the dead tore at his heart. *He stalks every family . . . our oldest . . . our youngest . . .* the words repeated themselves in Walker's mind. Who else was dying? Walker's frightened thoughts raced with his feet. Great Owl? Singing Woman? Morning Flower's newborn daughter? Walker's throat tightened in fear.

Nearing the first group of cliff dwellings, they could hear the sounds of mournful crying. White Badger and Walker slowed their pace to a fast walk. The usually busy path was desolate, abandoned. The smell of death swirled out of the first and third doors.

White Badger's feet moved faster. At the next set of homes, the intonation of a grieving song reached Walker's ears. The sorrowful words were almost exactly the same ones that he had sung at his Uncle's death. Walker's throat constricted so much that he couldn't swallow.

The trail seemed to go on forever. The minutes seemed like years. Death and fear drifted in the air like a mist of fog. Drawing near Great Owl's home, Walker's feet felt as if they were lead.

Son of Great Bear met them at his door. His face was

ashen and pinched in the harsh sunlight. "White Badger, it is good you are back. Many of our people are dying, dying fast." He looked toward Walker. "Gray Wolf is crying witchcraft to anyone that will listen."

"We will deal with that when we must. Our family?" White Badger asked, his voice laced tight with fear.

"Great Owl and Flute Maiden are out doing what they can for the others in the village," Son of Great Bear reported. "Morning Flower and the baby are doing well, so far. But Small Cub . . ." His voice broke, and his shoulders heaved. "He's sick, so sick that I don't know if . . ."

White Badger put his arms around his brother-in-law and held him close. Walker could see enormous pain in his eyes as he hugged Son of Great Bear. The aching pain tightened Walker's throat so hard that it seemed air couldn't get through. Tears pricked his eyes.

"He's at Great Owl's fire," Son of Great Bear said, easing out of White Badger's arms. He wiped his eyes with the back of his hand. "Flute Maiden said it would be best to keep him separated from Morning Flower and the baby. Morning Flower didn't want to be parted from him, but Flute Maiden was firm. Tag is inside with him now."

At the mention of Tag's name, Walker's heart flip-flopped with relief. He turned, took three quick steps, placed his hands on the stone ledges, stooped, and crawled into Great Owl's home.

The smell of diarrhea, vomit, and death met his nose. His empty stomach reeled. His head began to swirl. Walker held his breath and struggled to see in the dim light.

Tag knelt by Small Cub, who was lying near the small cooking fire. Tag was wiping the sick child's head with a wet cloth. Hearing Walker's footstep, he looked up.

His freckles stood out on his pale, worried face. "Walker! Boy, am I glad you're back. Small Cub is . . ." Tag gulped, unable to continue.

Walker crossed and knelt beside Tag. Small Cub's little face burned with fever; beads of sweat stood on his forehead. His eyes were closed. Walker stroked the boy's hot, sunken cheek. He groaned and turned his head away, mumbling indistinguishable words.

"Flute Maiden left some kind of medicine and some tea. He can't hold it down, or it goes right through him." Tag's voice was almost panicked. "I think he's getting dehydrated. Walker, he could die just because we don't know what to do."

Walker placed his hand on his friend's shoulder. "We will do what we can."

White Badger and Son of Great Bear entered the room. They knelt down beside Small Cub. Son of Great Bear reached out and smoothed his son's black hair. "We're here," he whispered, "but you have to fight hard, my son."

The worried look on Son of Great Bear's face and the love in his voice tore at Walker's heart. The memory of Náat's death was too close. How was he going to bear this? He closed his eyes to shut everything out. Silence filled the room.

"Great Taawa," Walker prayed silently. "Bless this child. Touch him and take this sickness from his frail body." Warm tears slid down Walker's cheek. "Taawa, guide me. Guide my thoughts that I might help these people that I have grown to love."

His already light head began to swirl with the mysterious, haunting feeling. Walker fought to remain conscious as a deep darkness threatened to overtake his mind. *Taawa . . .*

*Taawa,* he repeated over and over again in his thoughts, focusing on the word.

In the darkness of Walker's pleading mind, shadowy images began to form. He couldn't make out the scene being played in his mind. He forced his entire being into concentration. "You must learn the bahana's ways so that you can help your people survive . . ." Náat's long-ago words broke through the shadows. Walker's mind slowly began to comprehend as the darkness dissolved into light and understanding.

"Yes, of course!" the sound of his own firm voice startled him. He opened his eyes. His heart was pounding against his chest, and his head thundered with pain, but his thoughts were clear. He felt all eyes on him.

"Walker, what is it? You saw something again, didn't you?" Tag asked. His eyes were wide with anxiety.

"Yes. Yes! I know what must be done. It's the water, Tag. The disease is being spread through the water and the waste from the sick ones."

Understanding washed over Tag's grimy face. "It could be. It just could be," his voice was low. Thinking over what had been said, he exclaimed, "If it is that, then there is a chance we can beat it!"

Switching languages, Walker said, "White Badger, you must go and find Flute Maiden and Great Owl. Bring them back here as soon as . . ."

"We are here," Flute Maiden's voice came from behind them.

Walker turned to see Flute Maiden helping Great Owl through the low door. Walker rose to meet them. "I know that you are doing all that you know how to for the sick ones," Walker said, looking down into Flute Maiden's worried face. His heart tightened and yet softened at the same time. He wanted to gently touch her soft cheek, to hold her in his arms, and to shield her from all pain around them. Struggling to push these awkward feelings aside, he continued. "There is more that can and must be done if any of our people are to survive."

White Badger and Son of Great Bear now stood next to Walker listening. He turned to them. "Plenty of water must be brought up for each household. It must be put over a fire and boiled—boiled hard, before anyone drinks or cooks with it," Walker's words were tumbling out. "There must be enough boiled water for everyone to clean their hands with yucca soap and water after touching anything from a sick one. They must also always wash again before eating anything."

Flute Maiden nodded her head, "Yes, it makes good sense."

Walker saw the look of concern on White Badger's and Son of Great Bear's faces. "I know how little water there is and how hard it will be to get that much water to each home," Walker rushed on, "but it must be done. It is the only chance that we have to stop the spread of the sickness."

"My medicines and teas must be re-mixed using boiled water," said Flute Maiden, thinking out loud.

Taking it a step further, Walker said, "The old must be destroyed."

"Yes," Flute Maiden agreed.

Walker went on, "All refuse from the sick—the vomit, feces, and urine—must be carried out of the homes and buried deep in the ground. It must be buried far away from the village and from any water source. The same must be done with all waste from everyone." He looked into the faces around him. He knew that he had gone beyond their comprehension in asking them to do such difficult and strange things. A feeling of desperation flashed through him. *How can I make them understand it all?*

"It all makes sense and it must done," Flute Maiden stated firmly with authority.

Relief surged through Walker. He gave her a thank-you smile. He went on, "The meat that we killed today . . ."

"You brought fresh meat?" Flute Maiden interrupted.

"Yes, rabbit and venison," answered Walker.

"Venison!" Flute Maiden's eyes were bright. "I can make a special broth with the liver and strong herbs. It is just what the sick ones need!"

Walker's heart filled with wonder at this remarkable and beautiful young woman. "The rest of the meat must be divided among all the people. It will help fortify those that aren't sick. They are going to need all the strength they have to fight off Masau'u," finished Walker. He glanced toward Great Owl.

Great Owl stood close by, leaning on his carved staff. His warm, penetrating eyes were studying Walker. A wise smile lay upon his thin lips. His old head swayed back and forth ever so gently. "It is beginning even before it starts." The old Seer's words were spoken so low that only Walker heard them.

•   •   •

Responsibilities were quickly assigned. Within the hour, Flute Maiden and Great Owl were administering fresh medicine and strong broth. White Badger and Walker took fresh meat to each home. Though the pieces were small, all were received with gladness and appreciation. Walker explained what had to be done to stem the sickness. He knew that what he asked seemed ridiculous and incomprehensible to the ancient ones. He could see it in their eyes as he spoke. But the overwhelming fear in their hearts made them willing to try anything to save their loved ones and themselves.

Tag stayed by Small Cub's side, caring for him while Son of Great Bear organized all the people into work forces. Everyone who was able and who was not tending the sick was put to work. A group of men and children were sent to gather what wood they could for the fires. Others were assigned to haul water. One area was designated for the burial of all waste materials, with one person in each household put in charge of this task. The uncontrollable fear and the feeling of helplessness that had filled everyone's hearts began to be replaced with hope and determination.

•　•　•

The leather straps on the two water jugs slung over Walker's shoulders dug deep into his skin. He leaned his body forward into the hill as he climbed up the steep path toward the village. White Badger was just a few steps behind him, followed by seven other men and five teenage boys, all carrying full five-gallon water jugs.

The words of a prayer song filled Walker's mind and heart. It was the song that the Kachina dancers had sung at the last dance Walker had attended at his village. It had been just a few days before he had left his home to come to this canyon. Walker was now centuries away from that day, but the Kachinas' prayers, seeking strength and good health to endure the hardships ahead, were fresh in his mind. He began to hum the song, letting the words run through his thoughts. The deep, resonant tune was carried in the hot wind to each man and boy on the path behind him.

Seconds later, Walker heard his humming echoed by

each of those following him. Walker's heart quickened. He began to sing the words. Supporting his song, the humming continued loud and clear. The canyon walls echoed with the prayer.

The strong spirit of humble people working together to fight off a dreaded enemy filled the canyon. Walker saw acceptance in most faces as he worked side by side with his ancient brothers and sisters doing all that he had said must be done. At most homes where he went, taking water and encouragement, he was welcomed with warmth and respect. Walker felt that almost every eye was seeing him differently now. He was perceived no longer as a witch but as a leader—a leader they could follow in this life-and-death struggle.

Every eye but Gray Wolf's saw him differently. Walker saw that the hatred in Gray Wolf's heart burned more intensely than any fear of sickness or death. He met Walker at his door with a snarl. "Your trickery will not work with me. I have been alone for many years, so I have no one to lose to this death that *you* have brought to my people." Gray Wolf stared at Walker with contempt. "Fear and weakness blind the other; they do not blind me. When the time comes, they will not be so willing to follow you. I shall see to that," Gray Wolf threatened with a deep growl.

# 21

Walker's shoulders and back ached from the long day of strenuous labor. His heart weighed heavy. He sat on a mat next to Great Owl watching Flute Maiden bathe Small Cub's feverish body with cool water. Small Cub looked so little, fragile, and vulnerable. His eyes were closed. His pale face had a deathly gauntness to it. Mumbling incoherent words, he thrashed his arms and legs as if he were running away from some fearsome beast.

With gentle, soothing words, Flute Maiden spoke to Small Cub as she wiped the sweat from his hot body. Walker could see the overwhelming concern and worry in her brown eyes. He knew she was exhausted but would not rest as long as Small Cub or anyone else needed her.

Tag sat at Flute Maiden's elbow, ready to help in any way. He had not left Small Cub's side for more than a few moments during the entire day. Even when Son of Great Bear had come to help with his son, Tag had stayed next to his small patient. Tag's face was drawn and pinched tight with worry. His eyes looked like two huge, dark freckles staring out of his tired face.

Great Owl's eyes were closed. His hands rested on his crossed legs. His thin, weathered body swayed back and forth from the hips up. He hummed a prayer song. The tune was unfamiliar to Walker, yet something in its sound sent an enormous sadness through Walker's body. He had heard just such a melody sung at many death beds in his village.

Small Cub's body stopped its relentless movement, finally drifting into a deep sleep. Flute Maiden sat back on her heels. She wiped her forehead with the back of her hand. She looked at the tired bahana next to her. She spoke to Tag in a quiet, firm voice. "You have been by Small Cub's side all day, caring for him like a brother. Now for your own sake, you must go for awhile. Get some fresh air. Go next door with Morning Flower and the others. Eat and rest a bit. Then you may come back."

Walker interpreted Flute Maiden's words. Tag started to protest. At the sound of his reluctant voice, Flute Maiden put her hands on her hips and gave Tag a look that he understood well.

"I'll be back," Tag whispered to Small Cub, stroking the sick child's flushed cheek. With his knees creaking, he rose and walked stiff-legged to the door. Reaching the door, he turned again to stare back at the small child.

Walker's heart twisted with pain at the look of anguish on Tag's face. He rose and followed his friend out the T-shaped door.

Outside on the moonlit path, Walker reached out and touched Tag's shoulder. Tag paused, his eyes riveted to the ground.

"Tag." Walker felt Tag's shoulders shudder, then sag.

"It is not fair, just not fair!" Tag's voice sounded intense, bitter, hurt. Staring at Walker, he continued, "It all seems so stupid, so senseless, so unreal. People are dying of vomiting and diarrhea." Tears slipped down his freckled checks and glistened in the moonlight. "Here we are, products of the twentieth century with all its vast medical knowledge and technology, yet we can't do anything for them!" Tag's angry voice echoed off the canyon walls.

"We are doing all that can be done under these circumstances and it has helped." Walker tried to keep his voice low and smooth, despite the feeling of frustration that was raging through him. "There have been only a few new cases of the sickness since the people started to use the boiled water and take the other precautions. Flute Maiden said these people are not nearly as bad as the first ones. Her medicines are working well on them. She expects them to recover fully."

"What about those that got sick first?" Tag's eyes glared in the moonlight with a hopeless bitterness.

Walker shook his head. "It was just too late to help them."

"What about Small Cub?" Tag cried, brushing the tears off his face. "Is it too late for him, too?" Sensing that Walker could not or would not answer his question, Tag pulled away from him. "Useless. I feel totally useless!" He threw his arms up into the darkness. "You know, it's all really useless anyway. History has already written these peoples' fate. They will vanish, just disappear off the face of the earth, leaving very little behind. What is left will be destroyed by curious bahana Sunday picnickers out for some 'good, clean fun'—knocking down the homes of some dead Indians." Tag's arms fell limp against his legs. A deep sob racked his body. Silence filled the night air.

Sniffing, Tag clenched his fists at his sides. "Anything the bahana vandals find in the ruins will either be carted off or smashed to smithereens." With a jerk, he pivoted around to face the darkened canyon. "There will be laws passed that will make it illegal to steal any ancient artifact or destroy any prehistoric site. But even with these laws, and people like my Dad fighting to protect what little is left of the ancient ones, it won't be enough. The money-hungry grave robbers will still come in, digging up every burial spot they can find, looking for the pottery that the ancient ones bury with their dead. Those thieving vultures won't care if the bones they are scattering and desecrating were once a living person—a person with a name who laughed and cried, a real, live person who had a mother, a father, a brother . . ." Tag gasped for a breath of air. He pointed a long, thin finger toward Walker. "There is not one thing you or I can do about it, Walker of Time. Not one thing. We cannot change a blessed thing!" Sobbing, Tag turned and stumbled down the moonlit path.

Tag's words rang true to Walker and filled his heart with an overwhelming despair that he had never known before. His heart seemed to pump this hopeless feeling into every cell of his body, even to his very soul. Closing his eyes, he drew in the cooling night air. Even the air seemed tainted, stale, oppressed with an inescapable death. He felt as if the walls of the canyon were slowly squeezing closed on him.

Walker stood in the middle of the path, his hands clenched in tight fists at his waist. He lifted his face to the great, yellow moon hanging in the star-speckled night. "Why, Náat? Why, Uncle, did you send me here?" he asked in a deep whisper. "Tag is right. Nothing can be done. It is already too late for these people."

Silence filled the air, the sky, the canyon.

Releasing his clenched hands, Walker let them fall to his sides. They dangled lifelessly. His body felt like lead. He turned to look down the path. Maybe he should go with Tag. They could just keep going until they got out of this canyon of death. There was nothing left to do here except help bury the dead. It would be better to admit failure and leave before the ones he had grown to love died. Flute Maiden's lovely face flashed through his mind. His blood felt as if it were ice. He simply did not have the courage or strength to lose another loved one to Masau'u.

The sound of feet hitting the hard ground filled the air. A chill raced up Walker's back. His scalp began to tighten, but not from fear. The haunting feeling filled his mind and body. Even as Walker turned, he knew what the approaching messenger had to say. He had just seconds to decide whether to escape with Tag or risk facing death himself.

The runner, a man he had never seen before, was trotting up the path toward Great Owl's house. The moonlight reflected off the tiny beads of sweat on the man's face and chest. His breath came in ragged pants. His eyes concentrated on the rocky path. Just a few feet away from Walker, he lifted his eyes. He jerked to a stop, startled to see a stranger on the path. His hands flew to the knife at his waist.

"I am a friend," Walker spoke in a warm but shaking voice. "White Badger, whom you seek, is in the home of Son of Great Bear."

Standing in a defensive position, the man stood clutching his weapon, unsure what to do next. After a few seconds, keeping his eyes on Walker, he moved up to Son of

Great Bear's door. "White Badger," his voice was low, his eyes never leaving Walker. "White Badger, it is Dark Cloud. I must speak to you." White Badger appeared at the door. Dark Cloud entered, leaving Walker alone on the path.

The mysterious feeling filled the air. "Now. Now begins what you were sent here to do," Náat's familiar voice whispered as if it were sung by the stars.

"What is it that I am to do?" Walker asked himself, the moon, the stars. "What can I possibly do?"

A deathly silence filled the rocks and cliffs of the canyon.

A minute later, Walker sat down next to Great Owl in his house. Great Owl's eyes met Walker's. From the look in the Seer's eyes, Walker could tell he, too, without having been told, knew that Lone Eagle had returned.

Great Owl's eyes searched Walker's. The old man's wrinkled face showed no emotion as his eyes seemed to probe deep within Walker. Just a few days ago such eye contact, such intense searching, would have made Walker squirm and turn away. Now Walker looked back at Great Owl without hesitation.

Great Owl's face softened. "Yes, it begins. You are ready. But your path is not clear. You must be careful at all times. There are those who would do anything to stop what must be done. Guard your trust always. There are those who will turn against you now."

"I will," Walker said, knowing Great Owl's words to be true.

"Now, I must go to our chief." Using his carved staff, Great Owl struggled to his feet.

"I will go with you," said Flute Maiden, starting to get up.

"No, my daughter. Stay here with Small Cub. What care Lone Eagle needs, I alone can give."

White Badger came through the door just as Great Owl was ready to leave. He spoke quietly to Great Owl, then crossed over to Small Cub and knelt. He reached out and stroked the dark hair. "Keep fighting, little one. We need you as a good hunter and a mighty warrior." Then Great Owl and White Badger were gone.

Tag tumbled through the door. "Is Small Cub all right?" He knelt beside Flute Maiden. Tag's dirty, tear-streaked face was pale. His hair looked like a cross between a bird's and a rat's nest. His eyes had a haunted, lost look to them. There was panic in Tag's voice, "I saw White Badger and Great Owl leave—I thought . . ."

Walker explained the situation to Tag.

The small fire popped and crackled. The shadows on the wall were still. The air was thick with smoke and sickness.

Tag stared down at Small Cub's deathly white face. Tag's body began to shake as if he were cold. Was Tag getting sick? The thought shot through Walker like a hot bullet. Did Masau'u have his fingers around Tag?

Turning to Walker, Tag said in a ghostlike voice, "I have the strongest feeling that this is the beginning of the end for all of us."

# 22

Walker, Flute Maiden, and Tag sat huddled together near Small Cub. Each was silent with thoughts, questions, and worries. Small Cub was lost in a deep sleep. His small body lay peaceful at last.

Walker tried to relax his tired body, but every aching muscle was tense. He willed his weary mind to float free from the present situation. Instead, it stubbornly began focusing with clear and accurate sharpness upon each incident of the last few days. He struggled to place each happening together in a meaningful way, as he would put a complicated jigsaw puzzle together. Nothing seemed to dovetail securely or logically. Something, some basic information that would tie things together, was missing. The present ceased. Only the past existed as Walker arranged and rearranged everything he had seen and learned, trying to piece things together.

"Walker!" White Badger's sharp voice startled him. Tag and Flute Maiden also jerked with surprise. Walker turned to see White Badger standing just inside the doorway. "Lone Eagle wants you now." There was something in White Badger's tone that made Walker's scalp tighten. White Badger's face was like cold granite, impassive and unfeeling. He stood rigid, his fist clutching the sharp knife at his waist.

What had happened to cause such a radical change in White Badger? A foreboding feeling swept through Walker. This was not the White Badger he had hunted with this morning or worked with side by side all day long. Something was not right. Had Gray Wolf gotten to Lone Eagle first and convinced him that the strangers were witches who must be killed? Was White Badger just obeying orders? Or had he turned against him as Great Owl had forewarned? Walker's heart began hammering against his chest. Keeping his eyes on White Badger, he started to his feet.

Tag broke the thick silence, "What's wrong with White Badger? What's happened?"

"Lone Eagle has sent for me."

Tag started up. "I'll go with you."

Walker shook his head. "I must go alone this time." He flashed a quick half-smile. "Tag, whatever happens, I think that you will be safe." He hoped that what he had said was true, but he could not be sure.

Walker caught Flute Maiden's eyes. They glistened with tears and spoke of some deep emotion. Anxiety, worry— or was it fear he saw? Flute Maiden lowered her dark eyes before he could read them clearly. Everything suddenly seemed unreal, like a hazy nightmare. What was really happening here?

The warm night air seemed almost too thick to breathe. As Walker followed White Badger down the narrow path, his heart thundered in his ears. His palms were as wet as his forehead and chest, which were covered with sweat. He felt the spirit of death reaching its bony, black fingers toward him.

*White Badger has turned against you!* the walls of the canyon seemed to whisper to Walker. *Push him off the next ledge before he leads you to your death! Save yourself now before it is too late!*

Fear, with its accompanying adrenaline, surged through Walker's body. Panic began taking over his mind. He reached up and touched the eagle pendant hanging on his chest. "Taawa . . ." he prayed silently.

White Badger stopped, turning to face Walker. In the moonlit shadows, his eyes looked like deep, empty holes, his cheeks sunken and fleshless.

*Strike now! Escape now, or die!* a cool burst of air from the canyon sang in Walker's ears. The rank odor of death swirled out of the nearby doorway. Walker's heart hammered, and his throat constricted. His knees felt weak, yet every muscle in his body was poised, ready to fight or flee.

White Badger pointed to the door. His hand grasped his stone knife. He waited like a guard for Walker to enter.

Walker clenched his fist into a tight ball. He drew in a deep breath of the death-filled air. Looking up to the stars, he whispered in a deep, desperate voice, "Help me, Náat!" His plea died in the stillness before it reached White Badger's ear. Yet in his heart, Walker knew that he must enter this house of death. He had to do what Náat had sent him to do.

Releasing his fists and moving toward the door, Walker looked again into White Badger's face. It was masked in dark shadows. "I'm sorry, my friend," White Badger said in a harsh, raspy voice, "that there is nothing I can do."

Walker realized that whatever was about to happen had been taken out of White Badger's hands. If White Badger, the Warrior Chief, could not help him, no one could. He was totally on his own now. Walker tried to swallow the fear knotted in his throat but found he couldn't even swallow. He stooped low and entered the dwelling.

Great Owl was sitting near the center of the room with his back toward the door. Walker could see a small, seated figure, wrapped in a blanket of skins, hunched over next to Great Owl. Was it Singing Woman? Yes. She turned to whisper something to Great Owl. Her wrinkled face was pulled tight in worry, or was it grief? With uncertain feet, Walker took another step into the room. The low sound of a man's weak voice floated like smoke toward him. Walker realized it had to be Lone Eagle's voice that he was hearing. He stopped, trying to make out the words.

The haunting feeling washed over Walker, and he swayed on his feet. Again the low tones of the strangely familiar voice reached his ears. The feeling sucked at him, like a giant whirlpool pulling him deeper and deeper. His hands battled their way up to his pendant. Grasping it as he would a life line, Walker fought to stay conscious.

"Walker," Great Owl's stern voice reached through the encroaching darkness that was pulling at him.

Walker's eyes were blurred. It took every ounce of strength for him to concentrate on Great Owl's voice. He was guided by it as a ship is guided by the moans of a foghorn in a thick fog.

He felt Great Owl's dry, leaflike hand on his arm. At the old Seer's touch, air finally reached his lungs. The ferocious pounding of his heart slowed. Walker's eyes and head began to clear.

Great Owl stood in front of him, holding Walker's tensed arms. Great Owl's face was calm, his eyes shining. "You must sit." He turned so that Walker could see a man, who had to be Lone Eagle, lying in a bed of furs on the floor.

Walker dropped to the hard ground. Lone Eagle's face was hidden in the shadows of his fur coverings. With a slow, determined movement, a dark, wrinkled hand raised out of the skins. "Come closer," his low voice held great authority.

At the sound of the words, the haunting feeling again threatened to overcome Walker. He strained to keep his eyes in focus, moving his leaden body next to Lone Eagle, who was struggling to sit up.

The small fire nearby flickered and brightened as if it had been suddenly fed. The shadows over Lone Eagle's face faded away. The overpowering feeling broke over Walker like a violent thunderstorm, leaving him shaking to the quick.

"Qeni Wayma, Walker of Time," Lone Eagle's warm voice said, reaching through the raging storm to Walker. "Welcome home, my son."

". . . my son." The words filled Walker's panic-stricken heart with calmness. The magical veil that had hidden Walker's memories for so many years slipped away. The haunting feeling dissolved into sweet, warm memories of this home and this kind and loving man.

With tears blurring his vision, Walker slipped into Lone Eagle's open arms. "Father!"

# 23

"This is incredible!" exclaimed Tag, his tired eyes now wide. He and Walker sat at Great Owl's fire. "I can't believe it!" He shook his head, his tangled hair looking like an abandoned hawk's nest.

Great Owl had stayed with Lone Eagle, and White Badger was next door with Son of Great Bear. Flute Maiden, sensing Walker's need to talk to his friend alone, had excused herself to go check on Morning Flower and the baby. She had kept her eyes lowered, never letting them meet Walker's, as she quickly left. Walker appreciated her kindness. He was not sure he could have looked into her face and read what was written there. He had to first sort things out in his own mind and heart. He needed time to totally accept what lay ahead of him.

Tag rubbed his chin with a dirty hand, leaving smudges on his face. "It is all amazing. Unbelievable actually." He paused, looking around at the one-room dwelling, the mat-covered floor where he sat, the small, flickering fire in front of him, and the sick child sleeping next to him. With a wide, sweeping motion of his hand, he continued, "Actually all of this, not to mention just being here, is totally unbelievable. So what you just told me should make perfect sense."

Walker smiled at Tag. He knew that Tag was having as difficult a time as he had had comprehending and accepting what had happened—as he still was having, in some ways.

"Okay. Let me make sure I got it all," Tag stated. He pinched his lips together, thinking. "Years ago when your uncle, Náat, was a young man, he came here to Walnut Canyon looking for eaglets. It started to storm, so he took refuge in the same cave we did. Zammie! Somehow he was zapped back here the same way we were."

Walker nodded. "Yes, but this was many years ago. Great Owl and Lone Eagle were also young men then."

"Sounds logical to me," Tag said, pumping his head. "He starts to climb down from the cave but falls, gashing his head and hurting his leg. Boy, it's easy to accept that part." Tag chuckled. "Along comes Singing Woman and finds him. Singing Woman is the friendly, blind lady who weaves the mats, right?"

"Right, but she was young and had her full sight then," Walker answered. Hearing Tag retell the story that Singing Woman had told him as he had sat next to his father seemed to be helping to confirm things in Walker's mind.

Tag shifted his long legs. "She takes him back to her home to care for him. Lone Eagle is Singing Woman's brother, and while Náat is staying there the two young men become very good friends. Since Singing Woman is of marriageable age, it isn't proper for Náat to stay at their house for very long. Once he is well, he goes to live with Lone Eagle's best friend, Great Owl. Great Owl's parents welcome Náat and treat him as a second son. This made Náat and Great Owl like brothers, right?" Tag grinned, as if he were pleased with himself for his own deduction of the two men's close relationship. "Before long, Náat and Singing Woman fall in love and get married. That makes her your aunt, right?" Tag paused, his faced screwed up in thought. "Don't aunts play a pretty important part in the Hopi culture?"

"Yes, they are almost as important as one's mother. It is the same here," Walker answered. He was sure that was why Singing Woman had been the one to tell him of his past, with Lone Eagle and Great Owl adding bits of information only when needed.

Tag ran his fingers through his hair, only to get them tangled in the matted mess. "Did Singing Woman say whether Náat had ever told anyone about where he had come from?"

Walker looked into the small, smoky fire. Only two small flames licked the air. "She said that they had been married many moons before Náat had told her about his home on the mesas. He also confided his secret to his close friends, Lone Eagle and Great Owl, but to no one else."

"I can see why. I am sure the others would have thought that he was nuts, or—or a witch," Tag said in a low voice.

"Some did," answered Walker, looking up at Tag. He tried to remember the exact words that Singing Woman had used in describing the situation back then. "Times were very bad. Discontentment had started to fill the people's hearts. They were no longer as one with the spirits of the canyon or with each other. The people's harsh, unkind words had driven the rain clouds away. Their selfishness had kept the snow from falling. Because of the many contentions among the people, the crops became stingy with their harvests. The deer and antelope grew tired of hearing the complaining and bickering. They and our other animal brothers and sisters left to find a place of harmony to live. The people's belts were cinched tight against hunger by the time Náat arrived."

Walker paused, reaching up to touch his pendant. It was easy for him to visualize Náat living and working here. "Náat taught the people many new farming techniques, which probably helped them survive this long. But even with this, some people whispered that Náat had appeared out of the air and was two-hearted." A cold shiver slithered up Walker's back. His kind and loving Náat had also faced the serious accusations of being a witch.

"Then for many years there were few babies born, and very few survived. Witchcraft was whispered louder. To make things look worse, Náat and Singing Woman, Great Owl and his wife, and my parents, who were all considered a family, did not have any children for years and years. Fingers started to point at Náat."

"This is all so incredible," Tag said, standing up, his knees creaking. He began to pace back and forth in the small dwelling as if to expel a sudden burst of nervous energy. "Then your father, Lone Eagle, was chosen chief." Tag stopped. Making a quick turn, he walked in the opposite direction. "After many years and to everyone's surprise, Morning Flower and then White Badger were born at Great Owl's hearth. A few years later, again to everyone's surprise, you were born to Lone Eagle and your mother . . ."

"Summer's Song. My mother's name was Summer's Song," Walker said. It was the first time in many years that he had said her name. Her kind face swept through his memory. He recalled the sound of her warm voice singing prayer songs. Her name had fit her well.

Tag came to an abrupt stop. "Do you remember White Badger? I mean as a boy?"

Walker nodded his head. "Yes, and Flute Maiden. She is just a few months younger than I am. The three of us were always together. I also remember Gray Wolf bloodying my nose many times." Walker shook his head. "He was a bully even then."

"That would explain why they recognized you," Tag stated, resuming his pacing. "But Singing Woman and Náat never had any children. I bet that really helped the witch-craft rumor mill." He plodded back and forth twice in silence. Walker watched his friend, knowing that he was trying to accept what he was saying. It was hard to comprehend. Walker remained quiet, waiting for Tag to continue.

"When you were three or four years old, sickness or plague hit hard. People started dying just like they are now." Tag looked over to Small Cub's limp body.

"Worse," Walker said in a low voice, remembering Singing Woman's words. "In a star's twinkling, Masau'u claimed all the elderly ones but was still hungry. Babies in their mother's arms closed their eyes, never to wake again. Children stopped their games and lay down, never to play again."

With tears in his eyes, Tag stood perfectly still, staring down at Small Cub. "I can really understand and accept that." He brushed his eyes with the back of his hand. With a deep sigh, he plopped down beside Walker. He sat with his shoulders hunched forward, gazing at the sick child. Gently he lifted Small Cub's hand into his and cradled it.

Silence filled the stale air for many minutes.

"Your mother gets the sickness really bad." From Tag's weary voice, Walker could tell his short spurt of energy was gone. "Just before your mother dies, she has a vision or something. She sees that you, her son, will some day lead her people. She also realizes that you could get sick, too. So she asks Great Owl to use his magical powers to save you." Tag searched Walker's face. "Do you think that she knew about him sending you with Náat into the future?"

"I don't know." Walker stared into the low flames. "She knew that Great Owl had seen the same images of me leading the people that she had. I think she just trusted him to use his powers in any way possible to protect me."

Tag thought this over for a minute. Nodding his head, as if he accepted it, he continued, "So somehow, Great Owl zaps you and your uncle back to the future, where you have been for the last eleven or more years, right?" Tag turned to look straight into Walker's eyes. "But how?" Even before Walker could shrug his shoulders, Tag answered his own question. "I know! I know! It's not polite to ask."

Walker smiled at his friend. Silence again filled the thick air.

"While you were living in the twentieth century, things here just kept getting worse with the drought and everything. With Lone Eagle getting old and sick, Great Owl brings you back here. And now things get downright dangerous. Tomorrow at the fort, in front of all the people, your father is going to announce that you are their new leader and chief." Tag shook his head. "It sounds easy enough. Except that Gray Wolf also wants to be chief and is willing to kill anyone who stands in his way."

"Yup," said Walker with a tightness in his chest. "You know, you're pretty good for a bahana." He winked at Tag.

Tag ignored the teasing, his face remaining deadly serious. "How are you going to prove that you are Lone Eagle's son? That is, without getting one of Gray Wolf's arrow's straight through your heart?"

Walker reached up and touched his eagle pendant. "It will be done," he said, trying to sound confident. Fear began pumping through his body at the thought of what he must do in the morning. Could he take on such overwhelming responsibilities? Would he be able to deal with Gray Wolf and his followers? He swallowed the growing knot in his throat. "Now, Tag, we need to talk about you."

"Me?"

Walker smiled. "Yes, my friend, you. You just happened to 'tag along,' into all of this. Like you just said, things are going to get dangerous. Tag, I value your friendship too much to have your blood on my hands if something goes wrong."

"But . . ."

"No, hear what I have to say. Then you, and only you, must decide which path to take." Walker took a deep breath, letting it out slowly. "Great Owl has the power to send you back into the future."

Tag sputtered, "What?"

"Yes, back to the future. I can't tell you for certain what lies ahead for me or my people. You, however, have the option to return home to your own time and to your own people."

Tag's mouth opened to speak, but nothing came out. Closing his mouth, he looked down at his hands that were clenched together.

After giving Tag a few minutes to absorb what he had just said, Walker continued, "There are two catches to your going back."

Tag looked at him. Walker waited for Tag to ask the logical questions. Tag just waited for him to explain.

"First, if you choose to return, it must be done soon—

no later than tomorrow before dark." Again Walker paused, waiting for questions. When none came, he went on, "Second, if you go back, Great Owl cannot guarantee that you will go back to the exact time you left."

Silence.

"I think what you are trying to tell me is that I may not end up back on the day I left," Tag said. Reading the expression on Walker's face, he added in a low voice, "I might not get back in the same year—or even in the same century?"

Walker nodded.

Silence.

"Walker, I could take Small Cub with me! Wherever we ended up, he would have better medical care than he can get now. I could get him to a doctor. I could save him, just like your uncle saved you."

"Tag, think for a minute what taking Small Cub out of this time period would do to him," Walker said.

"It was all right for you when your uncle took you."

"Náat took me to a twentieth-century environment that is similar to life here. The Hopi culture parallels this culture so closely that it even scares me. You yourself said going to our villages was like going back in time hundreds of years. There was no huge culture shock or adjustment for me. The languages are so much alike that even that was not a big problem. If you took Small Cub back to your way of life . . ."

"It would be too much for him to handle." Tag's voice held realization and disappointment.

Silence.

"I know! What if I go back just long enough to get some medicine, enough for everyone, and then zap back here with it."

"I'm afraid there isn't that much time left." Walker reached out and touched Tag's shoulder. "You must decide what is best for you and you alone."

Silence.

Tag nodded. "I'll decide before it's too late. It is not going to be easy." He gazed down at Small Cub. A tear slipped down his cheek. He brushed it away with the back of his hand. He turned to look at Walker. "What are you going to do if and when you actually become chief?"

Walker answered in a low but firm voice, "Take my people home."

# 24

Tag placed the last piece of wood on the dying fire. The yellow flames licked the new log as if it were an ice cream cone. Tag moved closer to Small Cub's mat. He reached out and brushed a tangled strand of long, black hair away from the sleeping boy's eyes. Small Cub's smooth, soft cheek was warm. Tag felt the boy's forehead; it was just warm, not hot. A feeling of relief washed over Tag. He closed his eyes and tipped his head back. "Thank you," he whispered. "Thank you."

Despite Small Cub's improvement, Tag's chest and shoulders felt as if a weight hung around his neck like a huge yoke. In the very early hours of the morning, while he could still see stars twinkling in the sky outside Great Owl's doorway, he had made his decision. Was it the right one? he wondered now, feeling burdened and depressed.

He opened his eyes. Tears blurred his vision. Tag wiped his eyes and tried to swallow the lump in his throat. Small Cub mumbled something and thrashed his legs about. Tag reached out and took his hand, holding it tight. "It's okay. I'm here," he said. Maybe Small Cub wasn't really getting better. The lump in Tag's throat grew larger.

Maybe he should ignore what Walker had said about taking Small Cub into the future for medical help. He couldn't just leave knowing that Small Cub could be dying. If he hurried, he could take Small Cub before Walker and the others returned from the meeting place. They had been gone only about ten minutes. It would take a lot longer to make Walker chief, especially if Gray Wolf had anything to say about it. He could strap Small Cub to his back while he climbed up the cliff to the cave. *He couldn't weigh very much,* Tag thought anxiously. Kneeling, he slipped one arm under the boy's shoulders, the other one under his legs. Gently, he lifted Small Cub up, cradling him close to his chest. "Come on, little buddy, we're going time walking," Tag said, trying to stand up.

"Ingu. Ingu," Small Cub called, his eyes still shut.

Tag's heart stopped. He hugged Small Cub tightly, resting his chin on Small Cub's head. "Ingu," he whispered. "Mother." This was one of the few words he had learned here. "Of course, you want your mother, just like I want mine," Tag said, his voice cracking. He eased Small Cub down on his mat and covered him up with the fur blanket.

Tag sat back on his knees, tears washing down his face. "Walker was right. I can't take you with me. You belong here with your family." He realized that he had been a fool to think that he could. With both hands, he wiped his wet cheeks, but his eyes were still blurry.

He reached for Walker's backpack, which lay nearby. Opening it, he fumbled inside, then pulled out the ancient paho and one of his sneakers. Walker had gotten their clothes out of the storage room before anyone was awake, explaining, "You are going to need these again back in the future, but wait till you get in the cave to change."

Now after just a few days, the clothes looked almost foreign to Tag. The shoes felt heavy and awkward. His bright T-shirt seemed foolishly garish. Drawing out his rolled-up blue jeans, he wondered how he could ever have thought that these stiff, scratching pants had been comfortable. They certainly would be confining compared to his loincloth, Tag realized, searching the pockets. He found his Boy Scout compass, and using his T-shirt, he polished the fingerprints off the metal casing.

"Small Cub," he said leaning down close to him. "Listen, buddy, I need to talk to you before the others come back. I know that you probably can't hear me, but I have got to . . ." Tag swallowed hard, trying to go on. "I have got to go back to my mom and dad. I want you to know that I will never forget you or your people." A sob shook Tag's body. How he wished he could stay to help, but he knew he couldn't for many reasons, some of which he didn't even fully understand. Maybe everyone did indeed belong to just one time and place. What about Walker? Where did he belong? He was caught between two homes, two peoples, two worlds. How could he give up either one for the other?

Small Cub mumbled something, opening his eyes for a second.

"Small Cub," Tag said, squeezing his hand, "can you hear me?"

The sick boy's eyes opened again. He squinted, trying to focus. He smiled weakly.

Tag's heart pounded against his chest. "I want you to have my Boy Scout compass to remember me by. I know it's not much, but it's all I have." He held up the shiny compass, so Small Cub could see it. "Look, it even has a mirror on the back, which comes in handy for combing your hair and stuff. I'll have Walker show you how to use the compass, so you'll never get lost." Small Cub blinked, his forehead wrinkled in confusion. He closed his eyes, drifting off to sleep. "That's okay," Tag said, placing the compass next to Small Cub. He reached up to smooth Small Cub's hair. "I'll just leave it here for when you feel better. You'll be the envy of every kid in the village, not to mention all the women who will want to use your mirror." Tag tried to chuckle, but his throat was tight with a huge knot of emotions.

·   ·   ·

Walker looked up at the gray morning sky. Thick, dark clouds filled the canyon, making it impossible to see even the rim. The low lying, pewter-colored veil held no desperately needed rain. Its sole purpose seemed to be to isolate the canyon from the rest of the world while suspending it in time.

Following Son of Great Bear up the trail to the meeting place, Walker realized that the ominous cloud cover was the same as on that first day here when he had started his journey in time. He remembered wondering then if Náat's spirit had been one of those dark, flat clouds. A cold chill shook his body. *Náat, are you among these clouds, waiting for me to join you in death this day?* Fearful anticipation surged through Walker's body. He was glad that Tag was safe back at Great Owl's home and that he knew what must be done if he did not return alive.

The path grew steeper and narrower. Walker knew that within minutes he would stand before his people. *Great Taawa,* Walker prayed silently, *guide my thoughts, my words, that I might accomplish what I was sent back to do. Touch my brothers and sisters that their hearts may be in harmony with mine.*

Walker saw the stone wall that surrounded the meeting place. The sound of thunder filled his ears. Or was it just his own heart pounding? Straightening his back and squaring his shoulders, he followed Son of Great Bear through the unguarded entrance.

Son of Great Bear stopped a few feet inside the walled area. Walker stood next to him. The villagers sat on the ground, huddled together in small groups facing the rock platform. Walker spotted Singing Woman, Morning Flower, and Flute Maiden, sitting side by side in the first row. Great Owl, dressed in his long, red ceremonial kilt and beaded skullcap, sat cross-legged next to Flute Maiden. Scar Cheek and his wife sat directly behind them with Arrow Maker and his family.

Walker recognized all but a few faces. These unknown men sat with families that he recognized. He guessed that they must have been the men who had accompanied Long Eagle to the sacred mountain. Would their loyalty to his father be transferred to him?

Walker's eyes continued to search the crowd till he saw Gray Wolf near the center of the fourth row. He sat ramrod straight with his head slightly thrown back and his arms folded firmly across his chest. He spoke to no one. A spear lay across his lap.

A hush fell over the people. In a wavelike motion, heads turned around. Walker felt hundreds of eyes fall on him then sweep past him toward the entrance.

Lone Eagle stood in the narrow entryway. He wore a knee-length white kilt. A brilliant blue, beaded figure of an eagle with its wings outspread covered the front of it. Lone Eagle's gray, shoulder-length hair was pulled back at the nape of his neck. His thin shoulders and chest were bare. Pain and fatigue had dug deep furrows in his pale, sunken face.

White Badger stood at Lone Eagle's side. Walker realized that without White Badger's help, Lone Eagle would not have been able to walk up the steep path to the meeting place. He also saw that the strenuous climb had taken a heavy toll on his sick father.

Thunder rolled overhead, filling the canyon with echoes.

The cold fingers of worry tightened around Walker's heart. "Father," he whispered, moving to Lone Eagle's side. He slipped his hand under his father's arm and felt Lone Eagle lean against him. White Badger moved back a step, letting Lone Eagle and Walker stand side by side.

"My son," Lone Eagle said in a low voice, "we will take only a few steps together. Then you must walk alone."

Walker felt all eyes on him as he helped his father to the platform in the center of the meeting place. His heart hammered against his chest. The scant twenty feet to the platform became an emotionally brutal journey that seemed endless.

Walker felt his father's full weight on his arm even before they reached the steps of the platform. At the platform, White Badger moved up from where he had been following to take Lone Eagle's other arm. Walker was grateful for his friend's help in getting his father up the three flat, stone steps.

Reaching the top of the platform, Lone Eagle stopped to catch his breath. His body trembled, and sweat beaded his pale forehead. He smiled and nodded at White Badger.

White Badger's eyes filled with tears. His face was pulled tight as he stepped back, returning the nod as if he had just received an intense, unspoken message.

Turning to look at Walker, Lone Eagle gripped his arm. "My son, time is short," he whispered. His love-filled eyes searched Walker's face as if to memorize its every line and angle. "If only there were more time for us . . ." Tears veiled his dark eyes just as the clouds had curtained the canyon. Lone Eagle squeezed Walker's arm tightly, then pulled his body up as tall as he could. Letting go of Walker, he took slow, unsteady steps to the center edge of the platform. Walker followed, stopping a few feet behind him.

"My people," Lone Eagle started. The strength of his voice surprised Walker. "It is good to see each of you after being gone for so many days." His eyes looked down into his people's anxious faces. "I went to the sacred mountain seeking answers to the many problems confronting us: hunger, thirst, sickness, and death. While I prayed at the holy shrines on the sacred mountain, the answer to my prayers came." Lone Eagle swayed a bit but regained his balance.

"Many harvests ago, Masau'u, the god of death, relentlessly stalked our hearths. He stole loved ones from each of you." Heads nodded in agreement. "Masau'u was quick to take my wife, Summer's Song. At that time my small son left our canyon to escape death. Now Masau'u has again entered our village, stealing many loved ones from us. At this very moment, he is wrapping his cold fingers around me." Gasps washed over the crowd. Lone Eagle raised his thin arm, his entire body shaking. Silence filled the meeting place. "In answer to my prayers, my son," Lone Eagle turned, reaching his unsteady arm toward Walker, "has returned to take his rightful place as your leader and chief."

Walker moved to his father's side. Blinding lightning raced across the sky, leaving the air filled with tense static.

Spear in hand, Gray Wolf jumped to his feet. His eyes glared at Walker. "There is no proof that this boy is your son," Gray Wolf shouted with a determined voice.

The air vibrated with crackling thunder.

Lone Eagle's voice followed the thunder. "He wears the eagle pendant that I created with these hands and wore around my own neck for many years before he was born. When he left, I sent the pendant with him that all might know him when he returned."

"Anyone could have stolen the pendant. It proves nothing!" Gray Wolf stated, looking at the people around him trying to gain support.

Lightning flashed out of the rainless clouds. Thunder bounced off the cliffs.

Staring down at Gray Wolf, Lone Eagle proclaimed, "But no one can steal a birthmark."

Whispering filled the air. Walker saw heads nodding in agreement.

Lone Eagle waited till all eyes were on him again. "My son was born with a dark red, half-moon shape on his left ankle."

Like thunder, Gray Wolf's high voice instantly responded, "We have no proof of what you say."

"I was there when the child was born!" Singing Woman's strong voice declared. She struggled to her feet, turning so that all could see and hear her. "Being his aunt, I helped Lone Eagle's son and only child into this world. I was the first to hold him in my arms. My eyes saw clearly then and I saw the mark that Lone Eagle speaks of on the baby's ankle. I knew that it was the mark of one who would walk with many following. Fulfilling my rightful duty as the infant's aunt, I named him Walker. In my heart, I can still see that mark." Pointing in the direction of the platform, Singing Woman stated, "Look and you will find that mark on the young man that stands before you!"

Walker reached down and lifted up the leg of his left leather legging. Somehow the red, moon-shaped birthmark seemed darker and more distinct than he had ever seen it before. The people in the first rows nodded their heads, confirming what they saw. "It's there."

"The half-moon mark is there."

"Singing Woman is right." The words spread through the crowd with lightning speed.

Lone Eagle raised his hand for quiet but began to lose his balance. Walker slipped his arm under Lone Eagle's to support him. He felt his father's hand clutch his arm.

Lightning brightened the darkened sky for an instant. Silence fell over the gathering.

When Lone Eagle spoke, it was with firm authority. "A father knows his own son, his own blood. I tell you that this is my son, Walker." Lone Eagle held up Walker's arm. "Now in front of you all, I make him your rightful leader and chief."

"No!" screamed Gray Wolf, over the sound of thunder. "No!" his bitter words echoed long after the thunder died. "He may be Lone Eagle's son, but remember that he vanished with a man that came to our village from out of the thin air. Everyone knows that man was two-hearted—a witch!" Gray Wolf raised his spear, shouting, "Since then this boy has lived and walked among witches, becoming two-hearted himself! He is the one that has brought death into our canyon!"

Whispers, fear, and lightning filled the air. The whispers grew louder and were accompanied by thunder.

Walker felt his father's full weight against his arm. He wrapped his arms around him. "You must sit down, Father," Walker said. Almost carrying Lone Eagle's weathered body, Walker helped him to the back of the platform. He eased his father down, so he could sit with his back against one end of the stone shrine.

"You must always walk strong, my son; walk with Taawa," Lone Eagle whispered. His deathly white face was etched with both love and worry.

Walker's throat tightened. He squeezed Lone Eagle's hand. "Yes, like my father before me."

Gray Wolf's screeching voice filled the air, "I will not be led by a witch!"

Walker turned his head in time to see Gray Wolf's spear soaring through the air toward them.

# 25

Walker threw himself across his father's chest as a shield. In the same instant, he heard the sickening thud of the spear's deadly stone projectile striking the shrine just inches above his head.

"Father, are you all right?" Walker whispered, pulling himself up. Lone Eagle's eyes were closed. His face was ashen and without expression.

"Witch!" Gray Wolf's shriek filled Walker's ears. He jerked his head around to see Gray Wolf bounding toward the platform, a stone knife clutched in his hand.

Rising quickly, Walker grasped the spear's wooden shaft and pulled. The shaft broke free, leaving its stone spearhead wedged deep in the shrine's mortar. Holding the shaft in front of him, Walker swung around to block Gray Wolf's knife.

"I will kill you," screamed Gray Wolf, thrusting his entire body toward Walker.

Again Walker used the wooden shaft to block Gray Wolf's knife. This time, he snapped one end of the shaft hard against Gray Wolf's wrist. The knife flew out of Gray Wolf's hand.

Gray Wolf grabbed the spear shaft and began pushing Walker backward. His hate-filled eyes glared inches from Walker's. Thick, wet spittle sprayed from his twisted mouth as he growled, "I will not be cheated again!"

Using every ounce of strength he had, Walker pushed against the shaft and Gray Wolf, desperately trying to keep his footing. Gray Wolf forced him back a step, then another, toward the rock shrine. Just a few inches in front of the shrine, one of Walker's heels slipped into the sacred sipápu hole. His knees buckled, throwing his back and arms upward. With the sudden shift, Gray Wolf lost his footing. His body fell down toward Walker. Walker brought up his elbow, smashing it into Gray Wolf's diaphragm. A lungful of foul air burst out of Gray Wolf's mouth. His body began to crumple forward. As hard as he could, Walker brought his fist up to meet Gray Wolf's chin.

Gray Wolf's head jerked back. Walker's other fist pounded into his stomach, bringing Gray Wolf's body forward. Walker dodged to one side. Gray Wolf landed stomach-first across the stone shrine.

Out of the corner of his eye, Walker saw White Badger and Son of Great Bear leaping up onto the platform. Before he could move, they had their spears poised inches from Gray Wolf, who lay stunned on the shrine. Their eyes questioned Walker.

Lightning zoomed across the sky like a long snake's tongue, licking at the clouds.

Trying to catch his breath, Walker shook his head. "Get him off the shrine and watch him." He moved to where his father lay lifelessly at the base of the shrine. Kneeling down, he lifted his father's hand and held it, looking at his father's peaceful face. Tears clouded his vision, and grief tore at his heart. Only hours after finding his father, death had stolen him away forever. *No! This can't happen. I need you, Father. How can I lead these people without you?* Walker's mind screamed in anger. How could he go on? A tear fell on Lone Eagle's still lips. Stifling the sob building inside his chest, Walker gently touched his father's lips, wiping away the tear.

"You must always walk strong, my son; walk with Taawa." Lone Eagle's last words filled Walker's mind. A deep aching rose in his throat, making breathing difficult. He swallowed hard, but the ache remained. Would it or the pain in his heart ever leave? He doubted it, but Lone Eagle's memory would always remain in his heart, too. As after Náat's death, Walker realized that he had no choice but to go on—go on to face what lay ahead, and with Taawa's help he would. Tears ran down his face. Walker stroked his father's cheek in farewell. "I will do what must be done, Father," he whispered.

Placing his father's hand on his stilled chest, Walker rose. Taking a long, deep breath, then letting it out, Walker faced his people.

Thunder roared through the air. Walker waited till its echo had died.

"Masau'u has claimed my father," Walker said, trying to keep his voice from breaking. He could feel his people's sorrow in the still, thick air. Walker saw tears on many of the faces before him. Great Owl's head was bent downward, his eyes pressed closed, his lips pulled tight. With her hands covering her face, Singing Woman's shoulders shook with sobs. Walker fought to maintain his control. "Lone Eagle did not fear death himself, but for you, his people, he feared. His greatest wish was that all of you might live. In order for us to escape Masau'u, we must stand and fight him together as one people."

He paused just long enough for the people to grasp what he was saying. "Gray Wolf has accused me of being a witch," Walker stated, looking down at his enemy who stood between White Badger and Son of Great Bear at the base of the platform. Gray Wolf's face burned with hatred. Only White Badger's and Son of Great Bear's spears pointed toward him kept him in place.

Letting his eyes move over the people, Walker continued, "I will ask no one to follow me who truly believes that I am two hearted. I will lead our people in unity and harmony, because only through unity and harmony can we survive all that lies before us. Those who wish to follow Gray Wolf may. It is your decision."

Walker paused, watching the people sitting before him. They began talking to each other. He saw Gray Wolf's face fill with a hostile smugness, as he stood with his arms defiantly folded across his chest. The hair on Walker's scalp tightened. Had he made the right decision in letting Gray Wolf live another minute?

Loud thunder quieted the talking.

"Before you decide whether you will follow Gray Wolf or me," Walker said, "you must know that I will lead you out of this canyon." He saw surprised confusion sweep over the faces of his people.

Walker went on, "This canyon can no longer support

193

us. Our water supply can not quench our thirst and now it brings death. Our stomachs growl with hunger because the rains do not fall on our fields. When the snows come, we will freeze because there is not enough wood to keep our homes warm. Masau'u has claimed this canyon as his own. If we stay here, we shall all die."

Walker's eyes rested on Flute Maiden. "If we are to live, we must leave the canyon as soon as possible. Tomorrow!" Her eyes told him that she would be by his side.

The people began talking to each other in worried voices. Some shook their heads. Others stared at Walker in disbelief.

"Our people have always lived here. It is our home. There is no place for us to live but here!" someone cried.

"No," Walker said loudly, raising his hands, gaining the crowd's attention. "There is a place for us, all of us, to go." His eyes moved from one face to another. He spoke with his eyes as well as his heart. "Northeast beyond the Sacred Mountain there are great, flat-topped mesas. It was there that Náat took me. It is there that we shall go to live."

"To the witches!" shouted Gray Wolf.

"To our brothers!" countered Walker, before confusion could start. He felt all eyes on him. "They are the same brothers that our ancestors lived with in the underground world before great Taawa created this world." Walker pointed down toward the small hole in front of the shrine. "Their forefathers and our forefathers climbed out of the sipápu together, into this the fourth world." He knew that everyone present had been told and retold this creation story of how all the people of the earth had entered this world from just such a small hole. Each person here accepted the story's truthfulness. He could see this in their faces as he continued. "Once they had emerged into this world, each clan went in different directions seeking homes. Our ancestors came here. Our brothers built their homes around the mesas in the northeast."

"Why should they let us live with them now? Why not kill us?" Gray Wolf demanded.

"They are the Hopi, the People of Peace. It is not their way to shed the blood of others. They are our brothers, and they will welcome us. There we will be able to live in peace and harmony without hunger and death stealing our loved ones away."

"It is a trick, I tell you. You will die if you follow him. All of you will die!" Gray Wolf's voice snarled. "I will stay here and be your chief. You must stay with me!" he screamed uncontrollably, shaking his fists toward the people.

Lightning lashed out of the clouds, followed by long, rolling thunder.

Walker looked down at his people. He knew that not all of them would follow him and that those who remained would die. Each person had to decide alone who to follow. Who, of all these people he had grown to love, would leave with him? Which ones would trust him enough to give up everything they had to go to an unknown place? Could Great Owl, Singing Woman, and the other old ones survive the long journey to the mesas? Could the very young?

Walker's knees started to feel weak as doubt began to cloud his mind. He could not guarantee that each person who followed him would survive the long journey. His heart beat against his chest. Could he handle such great responsibility? Who was he after all? He was just a fifteen-year-old boy who didn't belong anywhere. What right did he have to ask these people to risk their lives to follow him?

What kind of fool would even try to lead them the ninety treacherous miles across the barren desert without adequate food and water? The images of graves stretching from here to the mesas flashed through Walker's mind, leaving his body trembling.

Maybe it would be better for everyone if he just left right now. No one would stop him. White Badger or even Gray Wolf could be chief. Walker's mind began to swirl in dark shadows. Yes! Leave—leave all the overwhelming responsibilities and death behind. He would get Tag and they could walk time! Of course! Walk time back to pizza, jets, computers, and . . .

Lightning shot out of the sky, striking the stone wall near its entrance. Ear-shattering thunder shook the ground, vibrating through Walker's body.

Náat's voice seemed to echo in the deafening thunder, "Take your people home . . . Take your people home."

# 26

Thunder rolled off the rim of the canyon and came echoing back within the limestone walls below. The rainless clouds still shrouded the canyon, giving it an eerie darkness. Walker moved up the narrow path with brisk steps. Tag followed, throwing quick glances over his shoulder.

Walker reached the foot of the cliff and looked up. The climb up to the cave was even higher and more sheer than he remembered. "Do you think you can make it?"

"Sure." Tag slung Walker's backpack onto his back, staring up at the cliff. "It doesn't seem so scary now after all we have been through." He turned to face Walker. "How many people do you think will leave with you tomorrow?"

Walker shrugged his shoulders. "I don't know. Each person must decide. Those that can't travel now because of the sickness . . ."

Tag interrupted, "Like Small Cub."

Walker smiled and nodded. "Small Cub and the others

will follow with White Badger in a few days when they can travel."

"Walker, I am sorry about Lone Eagle—I mean, your father." Lightning lit up the dark, flat clouds in the canyon.

"When I looked into his face at the shrine, I knew that Náat had sent the red cornmeal of the dead for his burial, not mine." Sorrow welled up in Walker's heart and worked its way through his body.

Thunder filled the air between Walker and Tag.

"I feel like I'm abandoning you," Tag said, shifting the pack on his back. "It was the toughest decision I have ever had to make. I want to stay here to help you all, but . . ."

"I know," Walker said honestly. He thought about those dreadful minutes standing on the platform when self-doubt and fear had consumed him. He had been ready to turn his back on his people and run away from his responsibility. Then he had heard Náat's voice in the thunder and had again looked into his people's faces. In Great Owl's eyes he had seen confidence. White Badger's and Son of Great Bear's faces spoke of total support and faith. In Flute Maiden's eyes he had seen unconditional love. In that instant, he knew that these were truly his people. He could not turn his back on them. With Taawa's help, he would lead and guide them.

A bright flash of lightning brought Walker's mind back to the present. Tag was studying his face. He realized Tag's decision had been no easier for him to make, and it, too, was the correct one. But what would he do without him? Walker's throat began to tighten. He swallowed hard. "You need to be with your people, Tag. I hope you make it back to them."

Tag nodded. "Good thoughts, positive thoughts, that is

198

what Great Owl told me to think when I laid the prayer stick on the shrine. He also told me that as long as the conditions were right I could try more than once to get back." A grin spread across Tag's freckled face. "You know, I'd probably be disappointed if I made it back the first time."

Walker chuckled, shaking his head. Yes, he was certainly going to miss this friendly bahana. A wave of grief washed over him. He was losing one more person he had come to love.

Tag said, "Just before I left, Great Owl said something else to me—something that makes me think it wasn't just a coincidence that I tagged along with you."

Walker looked at him. Tag's face matched his serious voice. "He said, 'Now is the time for you to do what you were sent here for. There is much your people must learn from the mistakes of my people. If your people are going to survive, they, too, must learn to live in peace and harmony with each other and with Mother Earth.'"

Lightning licked the clouds. Thunder sounded like a long drumroll in the sky.

Tag stared down into the canyon. "Maybe, just maybe, there is a reason I was sent along with you," he said with conviction. "Whatever time period I get zapped into, it will always be here in the canyon. If the timing is just right, I could be here when the ruins are first discovered by the white men. I can help preserve them and the story they have to tell."

Walker nodded. Somehow he knew that Tag was right.

"No matter what time period I go to, I am going to help my people understand the importance of learning about the ancient ones—not only here at Walnut Canyon but all over the Southwest," Tag stated. "At Mesa Verde, Chaco Canyon, Canyon de Chelly, and at thousands of other villages, ancient people just like your people are struggling to survive. They, too, will mysteriously just vanish. My people need to learn why these civilizations failed, so they don't fail for the same reasons!" Tag stopped for a breath of air. His fists were clenched, his face etched in firm determination. "When I get back to my own time, I'm going to become an archaeologist. I am going to write a book about all this that will knock the socks off everybody!"

Walker laughed and shook his head. "I would just settle for hearing how you explain all this to your dad."

Lightning snaked among the clouds.

Tag grinned. "Don't worry about that. When that time comes, I'll just take him right down to Morning Flower's home. I'll show him my handprints that I left in the fresh mud plaster that the women put on after the baby was born. How can he doubt that?"

Thunder roared.

"Well," Tag's voice broke, "I—I'd best be on my way." He shifted the bulky backpack and stepped up to the face of the cliff.

A new sense of loss crept into Walker's heart. "Tag."

Tag turned.

Walker stuck out his hand to shake. He saw surprise in Tag's teary eyes.

"I'm glad you tagged along with me," Walker said, as Tag pumped his hand. "I will miss you." He pulled Tag to him and held him tight for a minute. He felt his friend's heart beat against his own.

*Taawa, be with this son of yours, wherever he goes,* prayed Walker, watching Tag scale up the cliff.

"Remember, think good thoughts, positive thoughts," Walker called up to Tag, when he had reached the top.

Tag looked down at him. "I forgot to tell you that I think Flute Maiden has a real big crush on you," Tag yelled down. "You lucky guy." He waved and was gone.

A cold chill raced through Walker. The final thread to the future was being cut, leaving him behind forever.

"Now, I will kill you," Gray Wolf's snarling voice broke through the deathly silence.

Startled, Walker pivoted to see Gray Wolf standing in the middle of the path just a few feet from him.

"I will not be cheated again!" screeched Gray Wolf, raising a large stone knife.

Walker had nowhere to go. To his back the path ended in a sheer drop-off, to his right was the cliff's face; to his left was a hundred-foot fall into the canyon. The only way out was past Gray Wolf. Fear and anger filled Walker.

With a deep animalistic growl, Gray Wolf rushed toward him, the knife extended. Walker bent his body forward defensively, his hands up. His heart pounded in his chest with such fury it felt as if would explode.

Gray Wolf lunged at Walker. Lightning hit the cliff just above them, sending electrical currents sizzling through the air. The ground shifted and shook with a powerful explosion of spontaneous thunder. *Tag has been zapped back,* realized Walker, as he was knocked against the face of the cliff. Gray Wolf's feet slipped out from beneath him. His body fell sideward, hitting the narrow path, and rolled toward the edge. Walker lunged for Gray Wolf. His hands grabbed Gray Wolf's right arm just as Gray Wolf's body fell over the cliff.

Gray Wolf's falling weight dragged Walker to the very

edge. He lay on his stomach grasping Gray Wolf's arm, looking down into Gray Wolf's terror-stricken face. Gray Wolf's body dangled in midair.

"Reach up with your other arm," Walker managed to say. His arms felt as if they were being wrenched out of their sockets. "Reach up!"

Gray Wolf's eye's blazed with fear. He swung his other arm up, grabbing Walker's arms. Walker's body jerked forward.

Walker pulled back with his entire body. He felt Gray Wolf working with him, trying to get himself up and over the edge. His feet must have found some footing because he came flopping over the edge with a sudden thrust, landing almost on top of Walker.

Gray Wolf lay panting. Walker struggled to his feet, his heart still racing.

"Why?" Gray Wolf asked in between breaths, looking up at Walker. "Why didn't you let me fall?"

The question shocked Walker back into reality. Why had he saved Gray Wolf? Why? The traditional ways taught that killing others brought only destruction to the killer and all those around him. Did this apply to a man who had repeatedly tried to kill him? Walker shook his head. His mind didn't have a ready answer, but his heart did.

"I came in peace and will take my people and leave in peace," Walker stated with authority, looking down into Gray Wolf's pale face. "I want no one's blood on my hands, not even yours."

He felt Gray Wolf's eyes burning on his back as he jogged down the path. Walker knew that he would again face Gray Wolf in battle—maybe not today or tomorrow, but some day.

•   •   •

Walker stopped, shifting the weight of the heavy baskets strapped to his shoulders. Flute Maiden stopped a step behind him. Seeing her beautiful face looking at him filled his heart with warmth and peace.

The call of an eagle echoed as it circled overhead.

Náat's words echoed in Walker's mind, "Take your people home . . ."

Walker looked beyond Flute Maiden to the narrow path leading out of the canyon. *A line of people, his people, climbed the path . . . Men carrying spears and bows with huge baskets slung over their shoulders . . . Women with small infants in cradle boards bound to their backs and young children clinging to their hands . . . Older children following their parents, stopping often to look back toward their abandoned homes in the cliffs.*

# Afterword

Today, at the Hopi village of Mishongnovi, on Second Mesa, the Water Clan's legends trace their ancestors to the ancient ruins found in a canyon that the bahanas call Walnut Canyon. Stories handed down century after century tell of a courageous young chief leading his people out of that canyon to settle and live on Second Mesa.

*About the Author*

Helen Hughes Vick is a teacher and freelance writer who has been widely published in textbooks and children's magazines. A resident of northern Arizona, Ms. Vick has acquired firsthand experience with the Hopi culture through long-held personal friendships. That, coupled with a compelling interest in research, resulted in this work.

**To obtain additional copies of this outstanding title by Harbinger House simply contact your local bookseller.**

HARBINGER HOUSE
*Books of Integrity*
TUCSON